BETRAYAL AND LIES

CONVENIENT ARRANGEMENTS (BOOK 4)

ROSE PEARSON

LANDON HILL MEDIA

BETRAYAL AND LIES

Convenient Arrangements

(Book 4)

By

Rose Pearson

BETRAYAL AND LIES

PROLOGUE

"Good evening, Lady Christina."

Christina's breath caught as she turned her head to see none other than Viscount Harlow bowing before her. Had he come to find her deliberately? Or had she merely been another face in the room, another young lady that he might seek to dance with this evening?

"Good evening, Lord Harlow," she answered, turning to her great aunt, who was watching the gentleman with very sharp eyes. "Might I present my great-aunt, who has come to reside with us this Season?" She smiled hard at the older lady who, after a moment, caught the expression and dropped the severe look from her eyes. "Lady Newfield, might I introduce to you the Viscount Harlow?"

"How very good to make your acquaintance," the viscount said, bowing low as Lady Newfield bobbed a very quick and not entirely correct curtsy. "And you are Lady Christina's great aunt?" His eyes were warm, his lips curving into a genuine smile. "How very nice for Lady Christina to have such company with her in London."

Lady Newfield smiled back, although there remained that glint in her eye that told Christina she was still assessing Lord Harlow and wondering whether or not he was a suitable gentleman for her niece.

"I have been delighted to attend," Lady Newfield replied after a moment or two. "The Earl—that is, Lady Christina's father—is related to me by marriage. It was very good of him to invite me to London in such a way."

Christina resisted the urge to laugh, knowing full well the only reason her father had done such a thing was so that he might enjoy a little more time at his cards and other enjoyable activities while his daughter was being taken care of by the very respectable Lady Newfield.

"And you are here for the whole Season!" the viscount exclaimed, his eyes bright and shifting between Christina and Lady Newfield. "Then I am sure we will see a great deal of each other."

Lady Newfield raised one eyebrow, clearly aware of what the viscount was suggesting but choosing not to say anything about it. Christina felt herself glow with contentment, her smile ready for when Lord Harlow turned his attention back to her.

"Might I enquire as to whether or not you have any dances remaining this evening, Lady Christina?" he asked, his eyes filled with hope as she pulled her dance card from her wrist and handed it to him, choosing *not* to say that she had remained a little further in the shadows than usual, in the hope that he might have his pick of her dances. It had not been enough to escape the attention of some gentlemen, however, but there were still a good many remaining.

"Two, if that would please you?"

The way he looked up at her sent her heart racing. "That would suit me very well," she told him, aware that her heart was pounding furiously and yet forcing herself to remain outwardly calm and gently expectant. When he handed her back her dance card, she let her gaze drift over it quickly, noting that he had chosen the quadrille, and thereafter, the waltz.

Her heart turned over in her chest.

"I do hope that pleases you," he said, quickly writing it down on his own card before returning it to his pocket. "I can very easily exchange one dance for another if you—"

"I am very well satisfied. I thank you," she told him happily. "I look forward to our dances, Lord Harlow."

Lord Harlow inclined his head, his hands held loosely behind his back. "As do I, Lady Christina. Now, if you will excuse me, I will allow the other gentlemen near to you, for I am certain they believe me to be stealing all of your attention, Lady Christina, and appear to be a little displeased about it!"

She laughed as he moved away, seeing the smile on his face and feeling her happiness begin to bubble over. The quadrille was wonderful enough, but to be in his arms for the waltz was quite another! She could look forward to that delight with all the anticipation of a child receiving what would be a very precious gift indeed.

"A viscount, then."

Christina's smile faded as she glanced at her great-aunt. "Yes," she answered, wondering if this was, in her great-aunt's eyes, something that was a little lacking in Christina's choice. "I think him an excellent gentleman."

Lady Newfield's eyes twinkled, and Christina let out a breath of relief. Evidently, her great-aunt *did* approve of Lord Harlow's title, at the very least.

"I know that he is not an earl or a marquess, whilst I am the daughter of the former, but I do not think that a viscount is a particularly poor choice," she said, as Lady Newfield nodded slowly. "Father will not approve, however, unless I can convince him that I am just quite set on Lord Harlow."

"Then I must presume that you have particular affections for this gentleman, is that not so?" Lady Newfield asked, her usual blunt manner sending Christina into a spiral of embarrassment. "I must hope that you have more than just an appreciation for his handsome features, Christina! Do you know of his character?"

Christina nodded. "I do," she said, aware that, whilst they had not yet been courting, she had spent enough time in his company to believe him a very kind gentleman indeed, who was, in her opinion, more than suitable for someone such as she. "I believe him to have a generous heart, Lady Newfield. I think he treats me very well, indeed."

Lady Newfield turned her head and observed Christina closely. "But as yet, he has not asked to court you?" she said, and the smile fell from Christina's face almost at once.

"I do not ask you such a thing in order to harm you or to bring your spirits low," Lady Newfield continued kindly, "but only to assess where things presently stand between yourself and Lord Harlow. Indeed, I can see that you are very drawn to the gentleman, but I cannot see his responding to that emotion in the same way."

"As yet, he has not," Christina answered truthfully, even though the pain sliced through her heart as she did so. "But I must hope that, in time, he will be eager to speak to father and begin a courtship."

Lady Newfield nodded slowly, her eyes watchful as she looked into Christina's face. "You have great hopes for this particular gentleman, I think."

"I do," Christina admitted softly. "I find him to be utterly charming. Our conversations—although never of a particularly long duration—remain in my mind for days afterward. My thoughts are fixed upon him, reminding me of all and any interaction between us." She shrugged, aware that there was heat in her cheeks but finding that she was not embarrassed to admit it. "I cannot ask him about courtship, of course, so therefore, all I can do is wait."

Lady Newfield tutted, looking at Christina with one raised eyebrow. Christina laughed softly, knowing full well that her great-aunt was something of an eccentric who appeared to care very little for the strict rules of propriety. Most likely, if *she* were the one who was in this situation, then she would go directly to Lord Harlow and tell him directly of her eagerness to pursue courtship. That was not something Christina herself had any desire to do, however, and certainly was not something that she thought her father, the Earl of Enfield, would agree to either!

"You know that I cannot do anything else," she told her great-aunt, "even if you would not do the same."

"I certainly would not simply wait for a gentleman to decide whether or not he wished to court me," the lady replied, although she could not help but laugh at the look on Christina's face. "But, if you are willing to do so, then I shall swear not to say another word about the matter." Her smile faded, and she put a gentle hand on Christina's arm. "But do take care, Christina. Make certain that you know the gentleman very well indeed, that you are contented with him and that you believe he would be entirely suitable for you whether that be before courtship or during. There is no need to rush to any sort of decision. You might very well be filled with joy at the attentions of Lord Harlow but do not allow such an overwhelming emotion to cloud your judgment."

Christina nodded, looking at her aunt with a careful eye and wondering where such advice had come from. Had she seen such potential happiness turn to dust before? Or was this merely a gentle warning from a lady who had been wed for many, many years and knew precisely what sort of emotions now rose in Christina's heart?

"I will be careful, Lady Newfield," she promised, only for their conversation to be brought to a sudden end as another gentleman approached them, his eyes fixed to Christina's. Lady Newfield smiled at Christina, gesturing towards the gentleman as though to suggest that she had a good many more choices before her than merely Lord Harlow, but Christina did not take any notice. As far as she was concerned, Lord Harlow was the only gentleman worthy of her attentions, and she did not want to give them to anyone else.

CHAPTER ONE

"And how is your investment?"

Richard shrugged, his brow furrowing. "It is very difficult to say as yet," he said slowly. "To invest in shipping is something of a risk, although it might well bring a great blessing with it also." Nothing more was said for some minutes, allowing Richard to become a little lost in thought. His wealth, for a viscount, was substantial, and it had seemed wise to invest it in something such as shipping. However, he was still waiting to see whether such an investment would bring success, and that was becoming a trifle frustrating.

Viscount Prestwick clicked his tongue in annoyance, startling Richard from his reverie.

"Whatever is the matter, old boy?" he asked, a little irritated that he had been caught so off-guard. "Is there someone present that is a frustration to you?" He lifted one eyebrow, but Lord Prestwick only sighed heavily, gesturing to the other guests that were present at this little soiree.

"I find that I can see no one of particular interest this evening, Harlow," Lord Prestwick said, sounding quite forlorn. "I thought there might be, at the very least, one or two young ladies who could capture my attention, but it appears there is not!"

Richard chuckled, his irritation fading away almost at once. "You are being quite foolish," he told his friend, looking around the room and finding that he appreciated the many beautiful young ladies that were present with him that evening. "There is charming company to be found here. What can you be speaking of?" A grin began to spread across his face as he saw the slightly irritated expression of the viscount. "Unless it is that you were expecting a particular young lady to be present this evening and she is, thus far, not present as yet?"

"I do not know what you are talking of," Lord Prestwick replied, his voice stern. "I am sure you are being quite foolish, Lord Harlow. Sniffing, he turned his head away from Richard, but the action only convinced Richard all the more that what he had said was quite correct. Evidently, his friend just did not want to admit to it.

"Foolishness," Lord Prestwick muttered darkly, but Richard only continued to grin. "There is no one here who has captured my attention, hence my remark. That is all."

Richard lifted one shoulder. "Very well," he said in a quiet voice. "I shall say nothing more of the sort."

"Good," Lord Prestwick replied stoutly. "For otherwise, I shall have to begin to mention a particular young lady that *you* have been showing some noticeable attentions to. She is here this evening, I believe."

A swell of heat rose in Richard's chest, but he forced himself not to react.

"You are not going to entertain me, I see," Lord Prestwick grinned, clearly delighted now that he had the upper hand. "Very well, I shall not name her nor make any further remark—save to ask you as to whether or not you have any intention of courting the girl." Elbowing Richard, he continued to chuckle as Richard scowled back at him. "No? You shall not even tell me that?"

Letting out a slow breath, Richard looked up at his friend. "I do not think that such a thing is important to discuss with you, Prestwick," he answered slowly, finding himself quite unwilling to discuss matters of the heart with his friend. Whilst he had been jesting with Lord Prestwick, given he was a gentleman who was inclined to fall in love with one lady and then another a fortnight later, Richard himself was not such a gentleman. No, he was determined to keep his thoughts about a particular young lady entirely to himself, no matter what Lord Prestwick wanted.

"Indeed!" Lord Prestwick replied, now appearing to be a little affronted. "You are quite able to rib me about Miss Allerton, but you will not mention Lady Christina!"

"That is because there is nothing to mention," Richard answered with a shrug. "I will not pretend that she is not *very* lovely, both in form and in character, but as to what I have decided, that is not at all your business and certainly not something that I wish to discuss with anyone." A small twist of guilt needled his heart. "However, you are quite correct that I should not rib you and then be so unwilling myself." He cast a quick glance towards his friend, seeing the expectation growing on Lord Prestwick's face. "Therefore," he said, with a grin, "I shall not bother you in such a manner again."

Lord Prestwick's shoulders slumped, and he shook his head, a small groan emitting from his mouth as he did so. Richard chuckled and turned his attention back to the small gathering. Whether Lord Prestwick had noticed it or not, he had given the name of the young lady he was currently interested in, and Richard was eager to meet her if he could. It was always fascinating to see how Lord Prestwick behaved around such young ladies, for Richard knew all too well the gentleman fell in love in the strongest manner, to the point that no one could be compared to the person in question, only to then catch sight of or be introduced to someone who would then exceed the current lady of interest in almost every way.

"It is very difficult, I must say," Lord Prestwick muttered, taking a glass from the waiting footman's tray and taking a large sip of their host's brandy. "Finding a lady to wed appears to be much more bothersome than I had first anticipated. How is one to choose?"

Richard considered this question without mirth, looking out at the sea of guests and realizing just how many beautiful young ladies were present. Lord Prestwick was quite correct. Just how was he to choose only one when there were so many? And what was it about Lady Christina that made her a better choice than any other? His lips twisted as he continued to think. He could not pretend that there was no interest on his part when it came to Lady Christina, for she made him laugh and spoke with intelligence and wit that certainly made their conversations together very enjoyable indeed. Her beauty was undeniable, for with her dark raven hair and her sparkling blue eyes, she could capture the attention of any gentleman in the room. There was no reason why he should not consider her, could not begin to court her, but there was still something that held him back. Was it because he himself did not wish to consider such a thing? That he enjoyed the ability to do as he pleased, to speak to whomever he wished, and to dance with any lady he chose? Should he begin to court Lady Christina, there would be an expectation that he would draw close to her whenever they were in company together. This evening was a perfect example, for as yet, he had not made his way to her side, had not made any effort to greet her and converse with her thereafter. Was it that he enjoyed the distance he could place between them, whenever he chose? Or was it his lack of willingness to settle upon one living soul for the rest of his days?

"Good gracious! She is here after all!"

His attention pulled back to Lord Prestwick, Richard turned his gaze in the direction Lord Prestwick had gestured. He saw a young lady curtsying to their host, her fair hair in gentle curls piled on the back of her head. She appeared demure and, of course, elegant and gentle in her manner. Standing next to a lady whom Richard presumed was her mother, the young lady caught sight of

Lord Prestwick—and in an instant, heat poured into her face. Richard's brow rose. Evidently, this particular young lady was rather interested in Lord Prestwick—or perhaps she was merely reacting to his very obvious attentions.

"I think you have a young lady to greet," he said, elbowing Lord Prestwick. "Pray tell me that you have already met the mother, for she does look a little fearsome."

Lord Prestwick turned to Richard. "I have indeed," he said, with a triumphant smile. "And you are quite correct! Lady Peabody is something of a dragon. Thankfully, she seems to accept my company without hesitation!" With this, he strode past Richard, his head held high and his back straight, quickly making his way to Lady Peabody and her daughter. Richard could not help but chuckle, shaking his head to himself as he turned away, seeking to get himself another drink.

"Good evening, Lord Harlow."

Richard glanced to his left, a little surprised to see the Baron Fulham approaching. The man was small in stature, but from what Richard knew, had a great deal of wealth for his title, although there had been gossip about how he had come about such money. He was middle-aged, with a wife, a son who would inherit the title, and a younger daughter whom, Richard presumed, he had taken to London to try to find a match for her this Season.

"Good evening," Richard replied, not wanting to appear rude but certainly lacking any sort of desire to remain in the fellow's company for any length of time. "You are back in London, then?"

"I am," the baron replied with such a look of contempt that Richard almost stepped back in astonishment. "My daughter is to find a suitable match this Season."

Richard tried to look interested but prayed that this was not an attempt by the Baron to make him interested in meeting the girl. "I hope she is successful."

"My son, of course, is still unwed, but his choice must be much more carefully decided," the baron said with an air of arrogance in his words. "After all, he is to carry the title!"

"Of course," Richard murmured, wondering if the son was anything like his father and thinking that, if he was so, there was going to be a good deal of difficulty in finding a suitable young lady that would meet his standards. "Is he here this evening?"

The baron shook his head. "No, he is gone to Lord Melville's dinner party," he said, puffing out his chest as though this was much more important than anything either he himself or Richard could attend. "I am certain he is making an excellent impression."

"I am sure it will be an excellent evening," Richard replied, not wanting to say anything more and wondering how he might carefully extract himself from this particular conversation.

"However, my son does intend to enjoy himself whilst he is here in London," the Baron continued. "In fact, he is to join a game of cards tomorrow evening." One brow lifted as he looked towards Richard. "Would you care to join us?"

Us? Richard thought, narrowing his eyes just a fraction as he realized the Baron would also be there. Was this a game of cards set up by a particular gentleman? Or was the Baron attempting to corral various gentlemen from the nobility in order to make himself appear more important than he was at present?

"I—I do not think so," he said, hesitating. "I believe I am already engaged."

The baron did not look as though he believed Richard's excuse. "Is that so?" he murmured. "Well, that is a shame, particularly when so many other gentlemen will be attending—including your father, Lady Christina, is that not so?"

Richard stared in astonishment, having not expected the baron to speak in such an unseemly manner for one, drawing Lady Christina into their conversation in such a crude fashion. He turned and inclined his head, seeing the tightness in her expression as she regarded the baron.

"I do not know of what you are speaking," she said quietly. "My father's affairs are his own business."

The baron scoffed loudly at this, and a spot of color appeared on each of Lady Christina's cheeks. Richard found himself wanting to apologize to the lady, wanting her to know that he had nothing to do with this conversation nor the way she had been drawn in, but instead, he found himself quite at a loss for words, overcome with embarrassment.

"I am sure you must know when your father goes to play cards and the like, for surely he must ask you for your good luck and thereafter, tell you of his success!" the baron exclaimed. "I know that I speak of such things to *my* daughter."

"Whereas my father does not," Lady Christina replied primly. "Now, if you will both excuse me, I must return to Lady Newfield."

The baron, thankfully, said nothing more but, instead of bowing or making any effort to wish Lady Christina a good evening, merely turned his attention back to Richard, who was now both mortified and a little angry.

"You *must* come," the baron said insistently. "I shall send you an invitation this very evening, once I have returned home." He chuckled loudly as though this was something that Richard had eagerly desired to attend and was now finally being given the opportunity to do so. "I look forward to your company, Lord Harlow."

Richard closed his eyes and drew in a steadying breath the moment the baron stepped away. The man was odious, indeed, and he had not enjoyed a single second of their interaction. Watching how Lady Christina moved towards Lady Newfield, he battled against the urge to hurry after her, to apologize and to beg her forgiveness for something he had not done. Shaking his head at the baron's rudeness, Richard threw back the rest of his brandy and went in search of another glass. There was certainly no intention in his heart to accept the baron's invitation, no matter what the gentleman expected. After a display like that, the last thing Richard wanted to do was spend more time in the fellow's company.

"A pleasant conversation, perhaps?"

The gleam in Lord Prestwick's eye irritated Richard deeply.

"Baron Fulham is not a gentleman I should ever willingly converse with again," he said emphatically. "He was quite determined to have me come to some game of cards tomorrow evening, for whatever reason. I am to receive an invitation this very night!" He shook his head. "I believe the baron began by lying to me about the game, telling me that it was some gentleman or other who was to be the host, but I am quite certain that it is he and his son who have put the whole thing together."

Lord Prestwick tilted his head. "If you are speaking of the game of cards that is to be played at the Chadwick House, then I am attending tomorrow evening."

Richard stilled, looking at his friend in confusion.

"I believe it is the baron who has organized it all, yes," Lord Prestwick continued, "but a good many gentlemen will be in attendance, and I have no desire to miss such an excellent evening." He shrugged. "You will not attend?"

Richard did not know what to say. He had not wanted to go, had not intended even to consider accepting the invitation, but now that Lord Prestwick clearly indicated that he would attend, perhaps it would be a very enjoyable evening. Chadwick House was a well-known establishment, and Richard would certainly not be disgraced by his attendance.

"Perhaps I shall join you after all," he mused, as Lord Prestwick grinned. "It does sound like an entertaining evening."

"Excellent," Lord Prestwick replied, gesturing to a footman who brought his tray of glasses towards them both, with Richard promptly picking up a glass of brandy for himself. "Until tomorrow, then."

"I look forward to it," Richard replied, taking a sip of his brandy and letting out a long, contented sigh. It looked like this was a very promising start to the Season.

CHAPTER TWO

"Father?"

Christina opened the door carefully, peering carefully into her father's study, but was surprised when she saw it empty. A small frown knitted her brow, for she had been expecting to speak to him this afternoon before she took a walk with Lady Newfield into town.

Her frown still tight on her brow, Christina walked a little farther into the room, the door swinging closed behind her. Just where was her father? There had been some matters to discuss, he had told her, matters that he wanted to speak to her of before she spent the afternoon —and then the evening—out at various social events. So why was he not present? It was not at all like him to be so absent.

Meandering to her father's desk—and knowing full well she ought not to look at anything that was sitting there—Christina found her eyes drawn to a few papers scattered about. Her heart began to clamor, knowing her father was a very tidy gentleman and would never leave his papers in such a state. Her fingers brushed the papers, daring her to pick them up and, after a moment, she did so.

They meant nothing to her, she realized, her shoulders slumping. There was nothing other than numbers written on the page, and with them, a few scribbled words that would only make sense to her father. Sighing, Christina put them down again, turning back towards the door. She could not be late for Lady Newfield.

"Christina!"

The door opened just as she was about to reach it, her father framed in the doorway, his expression one of surprise.

"Father," Christina replied, a small flicker of embarrassment rising within her. "I was just looking for you." She smiled at him, but her father did not return it. "You asked to meet with me to discuss some matters that were on your mind before I went out with Lady Newfield."

For a moment, her father did not move. Then, he shook his head as though to clear it, before making his way into the room.

"Yes, yes, of course," he muttered, rubbing one hand over his face. "My apologies, Christina. It will have to wait."

Christina took a few steps closer to her father, only for him to wave one hand at her as though he knew that she intended to comfort him.

"I am quite all right," he said, sitting down heavily in his chair. "There is no need for concern, Christina."

Not quite sure she believed her father's words, Christina watched him closely, seeing the dark circles under his eyes, the weariness etched on his face...and then, she remembered.

He had been engaged last evening with some other gentlemen playing a few games of cards. No doubt it had gone on long into the night, and perhaps with a good deal of brandy and whisky with it as well. Little wonder that her father had been tardy this afternoon, and that he now looked as he did.

"When should you like to speak to me again, Father?" she asked, putting her hands in front of her and clasping her fingers together tightly. "Later today?"

Again, he waved a hand at her. "No, no, no," he said tightly. "It cannot be done today. Nor even tomorrow. I have other matters to deal with at present."

Christina blinked quickly, a little taken aback by her father's hard tone. "Very well, Father," she murmured before moving herself to the door. "I do hope you are quite all right, however."

"I am fine," her father replied firmly. "Now, go and enjoy your afternoon with Lady Newfield, and do not worry. And, Christina."

She turned, her hand on the door handle. "Yes, Father?"

His eyes were hard, hard lines between his brows.

"Do not ever come into my study alone again."

"You are quiet this afternoon, Christina."

Christina looked up at Lady Newfield from where she had been perusing a few new books. "I am?" She gave her great-aunt a small smile. "Forgive me." She did not say why such a thing might be, still feeling the stinging rebuke of her father's final words. She had not thought that she had done wrong simply by being in his study without his welcome, but evidently, she had done so. The way he had looked at her as he had spoken, the way he had behaved, all made her feel both ashamed and upset. It was not like her father to be so, and she had certainly never had any such thing from him before.

"Might I ask *why* you are so quiet, Lady Christina?" Lady Newfield asked, tilting her head like a delicate flower pushed gently by the breeze. "Are you unwell?"

Christina shook her head, trying to smile. "I have a few things on my mind at present, Lady Newfield, that is all."

Her great-aunt smiled gently, but her eyes still held a great deal of curiosity. "And what might they be?"

Finding herself entirely unwilling to say, Christina shrugged. The urge to tell the truth was not present as yet, the memory of her father's words still too harsh. Instead, she chose her words carefully. "A few things that would bring your spirits low, should I express all to you," she answered as Lady Newfield's gaze became a little more focused. "Let me assure you that there is nothing too concerning, Lady Newfield."

The lady studied her but did not immediately respond. It was as though she was considering carefully what to say next, just as Christina herself had done.

"Whatever it is, you know that you can share it with me," she said eventually. "Might I ask if it is to do with Lord Harlow?"

Immediately, Christina shook her head. "No, no, it is not," she said quickly. "I can assure you that this is nothing to do with Lord Harlow. In fact, I have not seen him in a day or so." Her heart did not feel any comfort at this knowledge, however, reminding her that her interest in Lord Harlow did not seem to be returned as yet. How long would she have to wait until Lord Harlow finally asked her about courtship? Her heart sank slowly to the floor. What if he would never ask her? Was she being foolish over him?

"You are quite correct," Lady Newfield murmured. "Your mind is plagued by a good many thoughts, Lady Christina." Her hand was gentle over Christina's. "Do speak to me when you wish to, my dear. I know I am your great-aunt and that we are not particularly close as yet, but I am here to listen to whatever you wish to say."

Christina nodded, smiled, but then turned back to look at the books she had been studying. Lady Newfield was quite correct to state that they were not particularly close, for she had only met the lady a few times previously. However, given Christina's mother had never been known to her—for the lady had passed away shortly after Christina's birth—her father clearly thought it good for her to now have someone such as Lady Newfield present for this Season. Although, of course, she was still determined to believe that her father had sought Lady Newfield's company so that he also could have some time away from the duties of accompanying his daughter through London.

The door chime rang, and Christina looked up, her stomach immediately tying itself in knots as she saw none other than Lord Harlow stepping into the shop. Had he seen her through the window and come to follow her? Or had it been nothing more than a coincidence?

Christina swallowed hard and turned away from the door, finding herself unwilling for him to see her. It was not something she could explain, however, aware that there was foolishness in her actions, yet finding her feet making their way to the back of the bookshop.

Breathing hard, Christina pressed one hand to her stomach and tried to reason with herself. Why was she behaving in such an odd way? Lord Harlow had always paid her great attention, and to try to run from him now made very little sense. Was it because she was frustrated at his lack of clear decision regarding their acquaintance? Or was it because she was beginning to fear that he would never seek to court her, and that her affection for him would die and wither to nothing?

Closing her eyes, Christina took in a deep breath and turned around slowly, thinking that she ought to return to Lord Harlow and greet him cordially, just as she ought to have done the moment he stepped into the shop. However, she had only taken a few steps forward when the door chimed again, and another gentleman came in, one she recognized but had never been introduced to. Spotting Lord Harlow, he moved quickly towards him, slapping him on the back and saying something in a quiet tone that Christina could not quite hear.

"Do be quiet," she heard Lord Harlow hiss, his words reaching her ears despite his obvious desire to remain silent. "I do not wish to speak of Chadwick House."

"Why ever not?" the second gentleman replied,

refusing to do what Lord Harlow asked and speaking just as he had done before. Christina found herself moving a little closer, although she picked up a book and half-turned so that her profile would not be seen. The thought that she was acting foolishly crossed her mind, but she threw it aside at once. Last evening, her father had been at the very same card game as Lord Harlow, it seemed. Chadwick House was precisely where her father had gone, and both Lord Harlow and this other gentleman had been in attendance also. Whatever had occurred?

"Because I do not wish to speak of it," Lord Harlow said, a thin edge of anger to his voice. "Have I not made that quite clear? Please, respect what I have asked you, Prestwick."

Lord Prestwick let out an exclamation of surprise. "You won a great deal of coin, Harlow!" he cried, his voice seeming to fill the quiet bookshop to every single corner and crevice. "Why should you not be pleased?"

Lord Harlow let out a long breath, and Christina could tell that he was growing angry with Lord Prestwick. She could practically feel it coming from him.

"Because, if you recall, Baron Fulham won a great deal also, and then appeared to be greatly upset with me when I refused a game with him to tie things up at the end," he said tersely. "Or do you not remember how he asked me to leave the establishment simply because I refused his offer?"

Christina pressed one hand to her mouth, a little surprised that, not only had Baron Fulham been involved in this particular evening, but thereafter, he had dared to demand that Viscount Harlow remove himself from

Chadwick House. The man was a fool to demand such a thing!

"But you refused him, did you not?" Lord Prestwick answered, mirth filling his voice. "And none of us present thought him in any way serious. We all laughed at his ridiculous suggestion, if I recall correctly."

"That may be so, but it did not remove the shame and embarrassment from me," Lord Harlow answered tightly. "And I believe that Lord Fulham was quite serious in his demands. The fool!"

Lord Prestwick made a sound of scorn, and Christina slowly began to move away from them both, hoping that they would not spot her. She had heard more than enough, quite certain that her father had not fared well last evening. That must be the reason for his strange melancholy. Perhaps he had lost more money than he had intended and was now regretting ever attending in the first place.

"Have you found something to purchase, Lady Christina?"

The quiet voice of Lady Newfield made Christina jump, quite certain that there was something of a guilty expression on her face as she looked at her great-aunt.

"I have not," she stammered, wondering if her aunt had seen her eavesdropping. "I am certain that I shall find something soon, however."

Lady Newfield's brows rose, her eyes straying to Lord Harlow and Lord Prestwick, who were still speaking together. "I see," she said softly, her gaze returning to Christina's face. "You have not spoken to them as yet?"

"I do not intend to," Christina answered, aware of the

surprise etched onto Lady Newfield's face. "Now, perhaps we should take our leave? Mayhap I will find something to catch my interest in another bookshop."

Lady Newfield frowned, her lips pressing together for a moment. "You are confusing me a great deal, Christina," she said, dropping Christina's formal title. "You speak of Lord Harlow as though he is the most wonderful gentleman in all of England. Your eyes shine, your cheeks flare with color. And now, when there is an opportunity to speak to him, you shy away almost at once."

Christina closed her eyes, fully aware that her behavior was, indeed, very strange, and realizing that she was not quite certain what she was doing or why. Her father's words had unsettled her a great deal and now to know that Lord Harlow had done very well last evening whilst, most likely, her father had done poorly, sent a myriad of emotions rushing through her.

"What is the matter, my dear?" Lady Newfield asked, her eyes searching Christina's face. "I can tell that you are not yourself. Is something troubling you?"

"Yes," Christina answered softly, opening her eyes to look at her great-aunt. "It is. But it is nothing of importance. I do not know why I am behaving so towards Lord Harlow, but mayhap it is because we have been acquainted for last Season and the beginning of this one, and yet he has not shown any intention towards courtship." She sighed and shook her head. "My feelings *are* involved, but mayhap Lord Harlow is not as worthy of them, as I had thought."

"Perhaps he is not," Lady Newfield replied gently,

"but there is also a chance that you are not being overt in how you feel, Christina. Have you shown him particular attention? Have you tried to make him see just how eager you are for his company?"

"No, I have not," Christina answered, honestly. "It would not be proper for me to do so."

Lady Newfield sighed ruefully and shook her head. "It would be *more* than proper," she said firmly. "Sometimes a gentleman needs a little more persuasion on the part of a lady before he is decided in his own mind what he shall do. Has it ever occurred to you that he might be afraid of rejection also? That he might fear that you will refuse him, should he ask?"

Christina blinked quickly, finding that Lady Newfield's words were only adding to her confusion. "I have never thought of such a thing, no," she answered honestly. "Perhaps I should..." She trailed off, looking over her shoulder, seeing Lord Harlow catch her gaze. Heat flared in her chest, but she did not allow it to stop her. Instead, she turned from Lady Newfield and made her way towards the two gentlemen, putting a bright smile on her lips as she did so.

"Good afternoon, Lord Harlow," she said warmly, turning to look at the gentleman next to him. "Might you do me the honor of introducing me to your acquaintance?" She smiled at Lord Prestwick, already aware of his name but waiting for Lord Harlow to make the appropriate introductions. Lord Harlow did so at once, but she did not miss the slight flicker across his brow as he did so. Mayhap he had not expected her to be either so forward or to be so eager to meet Lord Prestwick.

"How very good to meet you," she said, curtsying quickly. "I would introduce you to my great-aunt, Lord Prestwick, but she is, at present, in the depths of the bookshop."

Lord Prestwick smiled, and Christina found herself liking him immediately. He had something of a boyish face, and the smile that lingered on it spoke of easy charm.

"I shall be glad to meet her whenever she reappears," he said, glancing from her to Lord Harlow. "Have you found something of interest to read, Lady Christina?"

Christina sighed and looked at the books with a sorrowful eye. "I have been a little distracted, I confess," she said with a small shrug. "My father was a little weary today, and I am a trifle concerned for him."

Lord Harlow cleared his throat, drawing her attention. "I would not be greatly concerned, Lady Christina," he said, his lips curving in what she presumed was meant to be a reassuring smile. "He was with us last evening at Chadwick House. It was a very long night, with a good many card games, plenty of conversations and distractions, as well as—"

"And a good deal of liquor?" Christina finished, seeing what Lord Harlow had been so unwilling to say. "Yes, I suppose that might account for it."

Lord Harlow frowned. "He did lose some funds, Lady Christina, I will be truthful with you about that, but it should not be anything of significance to a gentleman such as he. I am sure he will be returned to himself come later this evening."

"I must hope so," Christina replied, her worry a little

eased as she spoke. "You are very kind to reassure me, Lord Harlow."

His eyes searched her face, and Christina allowed herself a moment or two to study him. His square jaw and firm nose, shock of dark hair, and eyes that shone with both brown and green were so familiar to her, but they still brought a shiver of delight to her frame. When he looked at her with seriousness, Christina felt her stomach turn over within her but chose not to say anything more, allowing the silence to grow between them for a few moments.

"It does trouble me to see you so deflated, however," Lord Harlow said after a few moments more. "You must not be anxious over your father, Lady Christina. Might there be something I can do to lift your spirits?"

This was a most unexpected offer, and Christina found herself unable to answer, looking up at him in astonishment. This was the first time he had ever said anything of the sort to her, and now that the moment was upon her, she could not find the words to answer him.

"That would be most kind, Lord Harlow," said a voice from over Christina's shoulder. "What is it you propose?"

Lady Newfield came to join them, her smile bright and her hand on Christina's arm.

"Shall we take a walk in Hyde Park, perhaps?" Lord Harlow suggested, his gaze still fixed to Christina's face, perhaps hoping that he might see a change in her demeanor at his suggestion. "Or mayhap an ice at Gunter's?"

Christina could not help but smile, her heart beating

a little faster as she looked up at him. "An ice would be wonderful," she said, as Lord Harlow's smile grew a little bigger. "Thank you, Lord Harlow. Already, I can feel my anxiety dissipating."

"Excellent," came the cheerful reply as he offered her his arm. Christina took it without hesitation, although her skin prickled and her joy grew with every moment. With Lady Newfield following behind, they exited the bookshop, leaving Lord Prestwick in their wake.

CHAPTER THREE

As much as he did not wish to admit it to himself, Richard knew that Lady Christina was becoming a little more important to him. When he had seen her at the bookshop, when she had shown immediate interest in Lord Prestwick rather than him, he had found himself a trifle irritated. And now that a sennight had gone by, he had felt that same irritation and frustration growing within him every time his eyes caught sight of Lady Christina speaking to any other gentleman. The conversation could be entirely innocuous, of course, but that did not seem to matter. It was as though he wanted every part of Lady Christina's attention solely for himself, no matter how foolish that seemed.

Whether or not it had been because he had seen the sadness in her eyes, the worry in her expression, or that he had felt his heart tug with sympathy, he now was discovering a new eagerness to be in her company. Something had changed within him the day he had taken her to Gunter's, when he had seen her smile brighten and her anxiety fade. He had seen her concern for her father and considered it to be yet another excellent characteristic— only to find himself beginning to desire that very same concern in her for himself. It was as though what he had been considering regarding Lady Christina was now nothing more than fleeting thoughts. She was quite the perfect young lady, with a beauty of spirit that he was convinced would always capture him. In fact, he had spent the last sennight doing all he could to be by her side, to converse with her and to dance with her. And this evening would be no different.

"Good evening, Lord Prestwick," Richard said before Lord Prestwick could open his mouth. "Pray tell me, is Miss Allerton here this evening?"

Lord Prestwick grinned. "She is," he said, looking at Richard with a sly smile. "And I presume the reason you are watching the door with such eagerness is so that you might be the first to spot Lady Christina."

Richard frowned, turning his head to look at his friend, only to look back at the door again. "And if I am?"

Lord Prestwick held up both hands in a defensive manner. "I mean nothing by the remark," he said honestly. "It is only that I have noticed your sudden change of heart when it comes to the lady. It is as though she has captured your heart entirely, although I cannot understand why, given you have known her for so long."

Richard shrugged, feeling the urge to be honest rather than hiding the truth of his feelings from his friend. "I cannot explain it, but that is precisely what has occurred," he said, as Lord Prestwick dropped his hands. "It is as though, in spending a little more time with her, outside of the ballroom or a soiree—just the two of us conversing—I have realized that there is a desire within my heart to be as close to her as I can be."

Considering this, Lord Prestwick began to nod slowly. "I can well understand such a feeling," he said, with such a note of tenderness in his voice that Richard looked back at him in surprise. Lord Prestwick was not watching him, however, but his gaze was fixed on someone just to Richard's right. Richard did not need to guess as to who it might be, feeling quite certain that it was none other than Miss Allerton.

"It may be new to you," Lord Prestwick continued, a smile now tugging at his mouth, "but I can assure you, it is quite understandable. And reasonable also, when one's heart is involved."

This remark immediately brought a frown to Richard's face. "My heart?" he repeated, having not considered such a thing. "I do not think that..."

Lord Prestwick chuckled, pulling his gaze from Lady Allerton. "Of course your heart is pulling towards Lady Christina," he said as though Richard ought to have known such a thing already. "You have an affection for her, which, I will say, will grow all the more now that you are aware of it." He shrugged as Richard continued to frown, having never considered that his feelings of interest towards Lady Christina might be a genuine affection for the lady. He had thought himself almost above such a thing, having been brought up to consider only a practical situation when it came to matrimony.

"Then, what do you suggest I do?" Richard asked, finding his throat a little dry as he suddenly spotted Lady

Christina walking into the room, with Lady Newfield beside her. "I am not certain what I should be thinking of next."

Again, Lord Prestwick chuckled, putting one hand on Richard's shoulder for just a moment.

"You consider matrimony," he said, dragging Richard's attention away from Lady Christina for a moment. "And what steps you need to take in order to be certain that such a situation would suit both you and Lady Christina."

Richard nodded but said nothing more, returning his attention to Lady Christina. She was looking all around the ballroom, seeming to him as though she were merely looking at the other guests, although part of him hoped that she was searching just for him.

Marriage?

It was, of course, the most obvious response to what he was feeling, but it was all so new and unexpected that his thoughts were pulling at each other, shoving to press to the front of his mind. Yes, he had been aware of Lady Christina for some time; yes, he had been considering her. But now that such a swell of emotions pulled at him, now that he found his heart was apparently involved with the lady, it was as though he had been set into an entirely barren land with no idea as to where he was to walk or how he was to survive.

Lady Christina's eyes caught his, and Richard found his heart slamming hard into his chest. The demure way she looked at him, a flush of color hitting her cheeks, had him almost desperate to go to her. But, of course, he remained where he was, not wanting to push through the guests towards her for fear that he would bring a touch of embarrassment both to himself and to her. He had to be cautious in all that he did, choosing his actions with great care.

"If you will excuse me."

Richard turned to see Lord Prestwick doing precisely what Richard himself had only just thought *not* to do. Practically elbowing his way through the crowd of guests, the gentleman made his way directly towards Miss Allerton, who appeared to be waiting for him to reach her. In a few moments, Lord Prestwick had Miss Allerton's dance card in his hand and was clearly perusing which ones he would be able to choose. No doubt, had he been quick enough, he would be able to dance the supper dance with the lady and spend all the more time in her company.

Then why are you not doing the same?

His feet propelled him forward before he could stop himself. Striding towards Lady Christina, his eyes fixed to hers, he barely saw the other guests, although he was certain that he had knocked into one or two of them in a most uncouth manner.

"Good evening, Lady Christina." Realizing that he was a little breathless, Richard bowed low and lingered for a moment or two in an attempt to regain his composure. "Good evening, Lady Newfield."

"Good evening," came the two voices together. Raising his head, Richard smiled at Lady Christina, seeing how bright her eyes were. Clearly, she was as glad to see him as he was to see her.

"Might I enquire about your dance card?" he asked, laughing as Lady Christina immediately handed it to him without hesitation. The eagerness that she felt was obvious in her manner, and Richard felt his heart swell with delight, all the gladder that he was the first gentleman to write his name on her dance card. Choosing first the waltz and, thereafter, the supper dance, he handed the card back to her and waited for her reaction.

He was not disappointed. Her eyes flared wide as she read his name, clearly aware that he had chosen two of the most intimate dances—which, of course, would be noticed by the *ton*. Gossip would spread in an instant, but he did not care. His interest in Lady Christina was firmly fixed now, making him regret that he had not done such a thing before. He had been foolish, waiting and lingering and considering his future with Lady Christina. Perhaps if he had examined his heart, he might have discovered her waiting there for him, waiting for him to discover the truth for himself.

"I hope they please you," he said quietly as Lady Christina nodded, looking up at him with flushed cheeks.

"Very much, Lord Harlow," she answered, slipping the ribbon of her dance card back over her wrist. "I look forward to dancing with you."

"As do I," he said honestly. Fully aware that another gentleman—namely, Lord Carrington—was eager to approach Lady Christina, Richard smiled ruefully at Lady Christina, stepping back with both frustration and relief. Irritated that he would have to leave Lady Christina's side when he had only just joined her, but glad that he had managed to secure both the waltz and the supper dance. Leaving Lord Carrington to speak to Lady Christina, he turned on his heel and considered whether or not he ought to speak to other young ladies and secure further dances. It would be all the more noticeable if he did *not* dance with other young ladies and only with Lady Christina, but that did not bring any particular difficulty to him. In fact, he realized, a smile spreading across his face, he did not particularly *want* to dance with anyone other than Lady Christina. What he had once considered something of an embarrassment was now all that he wanted to do. What did it matter if the gossip mongers noticed that he danced only with Lady Christina? Why should he mind if the rumors began about his intentions for Lady Christina when he was already considering his future with her?

Matrimony?

That word did not bring a sense of panic nor confusion to his mind any longer. The idea of having Lady Christina by his side as his wife was, in fact, something that brought a sense of anticipation. Courtship certainly now lay before them. All he had to do was find a time to ask her.

~

"LADY CHRISTINA?"

The way she smiled at him sent Richard's heart into a tumultuous roar. He bowed, offered her his arm, and could not help but smile with delight when she took it.

"How have you found the evening thus far?" he asked as they walked to the dance floor. "I am sure you have had every single dance taken by now."

Lady Christina laughed, turning so that she might

quickly curtsy before the music began. "You are very kind, Lord Harlow."

"But I am not mistaken," he told her, bowing. "Is that not so?"

"I do not think it matters," she answered softly, stepping into his arms. "For I have not looked forward to any of them as much as this one."

Her words seemed to unleash a flow of hope in his heart. As the music began, Richard held Lady Christina a little more closely and began to dance, their steps helping them to move as one. Richard did not say a single word, finding himself in such a state of bliss that there seemed to be no need to converse. It was as though a shadow had been lifted from his mind, as though he had finally seen Lady Christina as she truly was. He did not dare think what might have occurred had he waited for too long, only to see her courted by someone else. What regrets would have filled him then!

The music seemed to end much too soon, for Richard wanted to carry on waltzing, wanted to keep a hold of Lady Christina so that he might enjoy dancing with her for as long as he pleased. With great reluctance, he stepped back and allowed her free from his arms, seeing the small, rueful smile as she moved back from him.

Dare he hope that she felt the same reluctance as he?

"I know I am meant to return you to Lady Newfield, Lady Christina," he found himself saying, as she took his arm again. "But might you walk with me for a few minutes?"

Her eyes held a good deal of surprise as she looked up

at him. "Walk with you?" she repeated, clearly a trifle confused. "Through the ballroom?"

It was not the wisest of suggestions, of course, for the ballroom was very busy indeed and filled with so many guests that it would be difficult for them to walk together.

"We could take a short walk out in the gardens," he suggested quickly. "Lady Newfield would have to join us, of course."

Lady Christina laughed, and Richard looked at her in surprise.

"I am sure she would be glad of a short respite from the heat of the ballroom," she told him, her eyes twinkling. "But you will find that she is nothing more than a shadow behind us." Her other hand reached across and patted his arm as though reassuring him. "Lady Newfield might be a little outspoken and certainly brash at times, but she is well able to keep herself silent when it is required of her."

This brought a flicker of relief to Richard's mind, for having now decided what it was that he wished to do, he found that his eagerness could not be stayed. He had to find a quiet space for both himself and Lady Christina to speak so that he could tell her the truth of how he felt.

"Then let us seek Lady Newfield and ask her to join us," he said, praying that Lady Christina would not suddenly recall that she was to dance the next dance with another gentleman, making duty step in force her away from him. However, he had nothing to fear, for within a few minutes, Richard was leading Lady Christina out of the French doors with Lady Newfield walking closely behind them. Thunder seemed to rise in his chest as his desire to speak to her openly, to tell her of what had suddenly come upon his heart, grew at a feverish rate. He forgot about Lady Newfield, forgot about any other guests that were about him. All that mattered was Lady Christina.

"I must speak to you of something."

Frustrated that his words were unsteady, that his voice was not as strong as he wished it to be, Richard cleared his throat and tried again.

"What I mean to say is, Lady Christina, there is something on my heart that must be spoken aloud. Spoken aloud to you."

When he looked at her, her face was bathed in the flickering lantern lights, her eyes seeming to burn with flame as she turned her face towards him. He had never seen her look so beautiful.

"Please, Lord Harlow," came the quiet reply. "I will listen to whatever it is you wish to say."

Nodding, Richard tried to choose his words with care, but they began to flood out of him before he could stop them. It was as if his eagerness to speak as openly as he could had suddenly overcome him, forcing him to say what he had long desired.

"Lady Christina, I find that I am a changed man these last few days," he began, catching the look of aston- ishment in her eyes. "We have been acquainted for one Season already, and I have always found you...intriguing."

"Intriguing?" Lady Christina repeated, sounding a trifle disappointed.

Richard paused for a moment, trying to speak with as

much clarity as he could. "I have found myself drawn to you, Lady Christina, but have pushed such an emotion aside, believing myself to be uncertain about such matters. However, these last few days, I have discovered that my heart is filled with such an affection for you that it cannot be held back." He was speaking with more confidence now, finding both relief and hope in the words he spoke to her. "Lady Christina, I have walked into a room and found my eyes searching only for you. When it comes to dancing, I have cared for none but you. Indeed, I have known the gossip mongers will note my attentions towards you but have cared nothing for it!" With a small, wry shake of his head, he looked at her again. "I want very much to court you, Lady Christina. I know that it has been a long while since we were first acquainted and that you have every right to refuse me or, at the very least, to criticize me for taking such a long while. I am aware that I have shown you some attentions and have not progressed with them in any way, and you must forgive me for that."

"Lord Harlow?"

Richard let out a long breath, feeling himself now a little weak since everything had been said. Daring a look at Lady Christina, he saw that she was smiling up at him, her eyes seeming to shine with a joy that he had never once expected.

"I will not criticize you, nor will I express any sort of frustration," she said as they continued to walk slowly together. "Rather, I will merely accept your offer without hesitation."

It was as though the skies had opened and a bolt of

lightning had struck him, for his steps dragged, his heart pounded furiously, and his mouth refused to make a single sound. Lady Christina giggled up at him, making him shake his head to himself, trying to clear his thoughts. She had accepted him, and without even a moment to consider his offer! That meant that he had nothing to fear, no anxiety to plague his mind and heart. All that he could do now was look forward with joy to what next lay in store for them both.

"You cannot know just how happy this has made my heart," he told her, as she shook her head.

"No, Lord Harlow," she answered. "My happiness must far outweigh yours, for I have been waiting for what feels like an age for you to ask me such a thing." Her hand tightened on his arm. "Not that I have any intention of criticizing you, Lord Harlow!"

"You have every right to criticize me," he replied wryly. "I did not act when I should have."

"But you have acted now," she answered softly. "And that, my dear Lord Harlow, is all that matters."

CHAPTER FOUR

After what had been the most wonderful of evenings, Christina had eventually retired to bed but found herself struggling even to close her eyes. The joy that filled her heart had been much too overwhelming, for she had wanted to clasp her hands and dance about the room with joy, but of course, given it would soon be approaching dawn, she did not indulge herself. Rather, she had thought of Lord Harlow, thought of the overwhelming happiness that had filled her when he had asked her the only question she had ever hoped to hear from him. And, finally, sleep had dulled the edges of her memories, and she had found herself lost to slumber.

Opening her eyes, Christina looked around the room, seeing sunlight pour through a chink in the heavy drapes. The room was warm and made her want to snuggle back down under the blankets, to close her eyes for just a few minutes more, but the slight dullness to her head made her all too aware that she needed something to drink.

Tugging at the bell pull, she sat up in bed and pushed the pillows behind her, waiting for the maid to come in.

Having ordered a tray to be brought to her room, Christina let herself return to the moment last evening when Lord Harlow had spoken to her of his desire and his intentions. It was not a marriage proposal as yet, but a courtship certainly spoke to her of such a desire. She had never heard Lord Harlow speak to her in such an intimate manner before, and every word had brought a fresh joy to her heart, feeling as though she was walking on air beside him. Even Lady Newfield's gentle reminder that Lord Harlow had yet to speak to her father had not managed to dissolve even a modicum of her joy, for Christina was quite certain that she would be able to convince her father to accept Lord Harlow's offer, even though he was only a viscount.

Her father had never once said explicitly what he hoped Christina would achieve in her marriage, but she knew very well that it would be preferable to marry someone with a title equal or greater to her father's, but that did not matter to Christina. Her heart was engaged with Lord Harlow, and that was all Christina could consider. Besides which, Lord Harlow was a kind-hearted, sensible, and evidently, quite a passionate gentleman who spoke of his emotions rather than hide them away. That was of greater value than a mere title— at least as far as Christina was concerned.

Thanking the maid for the breakfast tray, Christina quickly dismissed her so that she might return to her thoughts. Should she speak to her father this morning? She did not know how he had fared last evening, or even what he had chosen to do, but if it had been another night of cards, another night where he had lost more than he had intended, he perhaps would not be as willing to speak to her as she hoped. A frown marred her brow. She would have to gauge his mood before she said a single word about Lord Harlow. This was too important an issue to rush into. Thus satisfied, Christina picked up her cup of warm chocolate and took a small sip, feeling herself refreshed and revived with even the smallest mouthful. A smile lingered as she picked up a piece of buttered toast. If all went well, then this very morning, she would be able to write to Lord Harlow to tell him that all was just as they had hoped.

IT WAS NOT her father's voice that caught Christina's attention, but rather that of another gentleman. And what made it all the more odd was that the voice was raised, speaking with such force and intention that Christina could make out every word.

Do not eavesdrop, she told herself sternly. *You know you ought not to listen at the door. Your father would...*

Her thoughts died away as she heard her father's angry tones, forceful and loud, throwing words back at the first. All thought of continuing on her way, of making her way past the study without even a moment of hesitation, flew from her mind in only a moment. Something— or someone—had upset her father and Christina could not simply walk by! Taking a few steps closer, she waited to hear the gentleman speak again, only for a lady's voice to now interrupt them.

"You owe us a great deal of money," came the lady's voice, silky smooth but with just as much force as the gentleman's. "And yet, you have not paid it."

"I shall!" Lord Enfield exclaimed, a sudden thump making Christina stumble back, one hand to her heart. "I am already speaking to my solicitors and I—"

"We do not care about solicitors," came the gentleman's voice. "We have already made the terms clear. Your vowels state that you will give us whatever we wish, do they not?"

Christina caught her breath, one hand pressed to her mouth. Had her father really been so foolish as to write something like that down on a piece of paper, and then to hand it to this gentleman, whoever he was? Her heart began to thump painfully in her chest, her stomach tightening with tension. Just what had her father done?

"I have no recollection of doing such a thing," Lord Enfield threw back. "I am aware that I owe you coin, and that matter is already being dealt with, as I have made quite clear."

A hard laugh came from the gentleman. "But as my wife has just explained, Lord Enfield, that is not what your vowel states. It is that you will give us whatever we wish in lieu of the money."

"And what we wish is to live in your estate for the next two years," came the wife's voice. "You may live there also, if you wish, but for all intents and purposes, it will be our home." A small but cruel laugh came from her as Christina's eyes flared wide with horror, hardly daring to believe what she was hearing. "And you shall give it to us without hesitation, Lord Harlow, else we may demand something else altogether."

Closing her eyes, Christina leaned against the wall, her breathing ragged. What had her father been thinking of in sighing such a vowel? Had his senses been so blinded by liquor as to make him foolish? A gentleman's word was his honor, and whatever her father had written was what they would now demand from him— but to demand Enfield House was quite extraordinary! What would a gentleman and a lady do with such a property, when surely, they already had their own manor house?

"Why should you demand this from me?" she heard her father ask, speaking the question that had been firmly in Christina's mind. "What is it that you hope to gain?"

There came a moment of silence, and Christina held her breath, suddenly afraid that they would peer out the door and see her standing there. But then the answer came, and she let out her breath slowly, her heart still pounding with a furiousness that seemed to capture her whole being.

"It does not matter what we wish to use your townhouse for," the gentleman answered harshly. "We might burn the place to the ground, should we wish to, and you would have nothing to say on the matter for you have already given us permission to live there as we choose."

"I have given you no such thing!" Lord Enfield declared, and Christina felt a swell of pride at her father's refusal to give in to what was being demanded. "I have never once expressed any agreement to this matter. I have stated that I will give you the coin that you are owed and—"

"No!" The gentleman's voice was louder now, filled with a fury that sent a sheen of sweat across Christina's brow.

"No, we will not have it!" he shouted, his voice seeming to press through all the tiny spaces in the doorway and make its way directly into Christina's heart, sending a tremor of fear through her. "We do not want your coin, Enfield! You will agree to uphold your agreement else, as my wife has stated, there will be consequences for your refusal."

Before she knew what she was doing, Christina found herself standing in her father's study, the door pushed open with one hand and her other hand curled into a fist. Breathing hard, she stared into the face of a small gentleman, with graying hair and a dark look in his eyes.

"Christina, what are you doing here?" her father asked, but Christina pointed one long finger out towards the man and glared at him.

"How dare you?" she hissed, her anger burning hot within her. "How *dare* you come into my father's house and demand that he obey you in such a fashion?" She stepped to one side, holding the door open wide. "Remove yourselves at once or else I shall have the footmen do so."

For an instant, no one moved. Christina's fury burned all the hotter, her eyes narrowing as she glowered at the gentleman. Whatever had occurred, she did not think that this man had any right to demand such things of an earl, especially not one as distinguished as her father.

And then, the man began to laugh. In fact, not only to laugh but to roar with mirth, throwing his head back as he mocked her relentlessly. His wife joined in, her hand pressed against her stomach as she bent forward, clearly making fun of Christina and what she had just announced. This only made Christina all the angrier, stamping her foot in sheer fury, only for her father to move towards her, wrapping his arm about her shoulders in a protective fashion.

"Christina, this is not for your ears," her father said, whispering to her. "I am trying to protect you from Baron Fulham." She looked up at him and saw the paleness of his face. "Why ever did you come in?"

"Do you know, Fulham," Lady Fulham said, her eyes straying towards Christina. "I think that this might be the perfect punishment for Lord Enfield."

Immediately, Christina's stomach dropped to the floor. The calculated look that came into the baron's eyes only made her all the angrier, although she could not help but feel a frisson of fear rattle through her bones.

"Indeed," the baron said slowly, looking from Christina to his wife and back again. "You have refused us too many times already, Lord Enfield. I am certain that we can find a use for your beautiful daughter, Lord Enfield." He chuckled, and Christina felt a shudder run straight through her. "I can see now why you did not tell us of her presence before." His eyes drifted back towards Christina. "We do have a *very* eligible son, after all."

Her stomach began to churn, making her realize that

she had ended up placing herself in a very dark situation, indeed. It would have been wiser of her to stay out of the study, to leave her father to his own business matter, rather than bursting into the room as she had done, but it was too late for regrets now.

"I do not care for your son," she stated, holding her head high. "In fact, I am already being courted by another gentleman."

Lady Fulham took a step closer to her, making Christina shiver under her cold gaze. "You are quite mistaken, Lady Christina," she said softly. "The only gentleman who is now courting you is our son, the Honorable Stephen Markham. Your betrothed."

Christina shook her head. "No," she said firmly. "I will not be accepting a courtship—nor a betrothal—from any other gentleman."

"You will do as your father says," Lady Fulham remarked, her smile easy upon her lips, although none of it reached her eyes. "And your father owes us a good deal of coin, which we are exchanging for something that we require—as his vowel states." She lifted one hand, reaching out as though to tip Christina's chin up as if she needed to get a better look at her, but Christina jerked back at once, her anger now slowly fading to fear.

"There will be no need for the estate now, I suppose," Lord Fulham said slowly, turning to his wife. "We only wanted it to increase our son's prospects, so that he might marry higher than his station." One shoulder lifted in a small shrug. "To state that he already had an estate of his own, which, perhaps, he had *purchased* from the Earl of Enfield, would give him great standing indeed." A look of delight spread over his face, which only increased Christina's terror. "But if he is to wed the daughter of an Earl, then I cannot think that we would need such a thing. After all, there would be an excellent dowry with the marriage, I am sure."

Christina closed her eyes. This was disastrous. She had no desire to marry any such gentleman and, after having had the joy of Lord Harlow offering his court, she could not allow this now to ruin her happiness.

"I cannot, Father," she said, opening her eyes to look up into his haggard face. She spoke very quietly and directly to him. "I have another gentleman eager to court me, and I have accepted him. If all goes well, then I think he will offer to marry me." She pressed her hand to her father's cheek, seeing the brokenness in his expression, how he could not meet her gaze. "Please, do not force me to do such a thing."

Her father said nothing for some moments, his shoulders slumped and his expression heavy with grief. When he did speak, his words tore at her heart, leaving her breathless with sorrow.

"I have no choice, Christina," he told her heavily. "The vowel is written in my own hand. I cannot see what else I am to do other than to agree."

"But you would not give up the estate," Christina pleaded, her heart pounding furiously within her. "You told them you would not! How can you so easily give me away to a man you do not even know? Whose father is a cruel and treacherous creature such as this?"

Lord Enfield closed his eyes and settled one hand on Christina's shoulder. She recoiled from his touch, finding no comfort in her father's side but instead feeling as though she was slowly being betrayed.

"If I do not abide by the vowel I have given, then it will be my death," he told her, his voice barely loud enough to reach her ears. "They will call me for a duel, and I shall have no other choice but to accept." He held out one hand to her, and she saw it tremble, her heart squeezing hard with a sympathy she did not want to feel. "There is no doubt in my mind as to the outcome, Christina, and I could not place the burden of being a second onto any gentleman that I know. And then what would become of you? What would become of the Enfield estate?" Dropping his hand, he looked into her face, lowering his voice all the more so that she had to strain to hear him. "I will do all I can to delay this marriage so that I can find a way to save you from it," he told her, giving her only the smallest flicker of hope. "But for the present, can you not see that there is no other choice for me but to agree?"

Christina shook her head—not because she disagreed, but because she wanted desperately to discover a way to free her father from this, to free *herself* from this situation. The more she thought about it, the more her mind became tangled and confused with all that she was trying to uncover. There was no simple way for her father to escape this. Instead, she had unwittingly placed herself firmly in the middle of this situation without any way of escape.

"It seems we have an agreement," Baron Fulham exclaimed as Christina dropped her head, unable to even look at him. "How wonderful. I am so *very* glad that it has come about in such a way. I should thank you, Lady Christina, for stepping into the study as you did and making us aware of your presence!" He chuckled loudly. "We might never have known of you until it was much too late."

"We shall make certain to introduce you to our son at the next available opportunity," Lady Fulham said, her voice filled with triumph. "Until then, Lady Christina, I think we shall take our leave." She laughed, the tinkling sound filling the room and rubbing raw over Christina's skin. "I am certain you will have a good deal to discuss."

"As do we, Lord Enfield," Lord Fulham remarked, his voice now a little lower than before. "I look forward to arranging the dowry very soon. And recall that you are not to say a word of our agreement to another living soul. The consequences of doing so, I can assure you, will not be worth it."

And with that, they left the room, leaving Christina and her father standing alone together in the quiet study. Christina closed her eyes tightly, feeling the hot swell of tears press against her lids as she fought to keep her composure.

"Oh, Christina," her father said, his voice broken by emotion. "I am so very sorry."

He stumbled away from her, pouring two glasses of brandy—one much smaller than the other—before coming back to press it into her hands. Then, he slumped in his chair, leaving Christina to stand alone in the study. She was shaking violently, she realized, seeing the brandy slopping back and forth in the glass. Her mind was a haze of painful thoughts, her heart slamming furiously into her chest as she stared down at the brandy, not quite certain that she had taken in everything that had just occurred.

"I do not know what else to say," the earl said, covering his eyes with his hands. "I am sorry, Christina. I truly am sorry."

Christina said nothing, her legs beginning to give way beneath her. Stumbling back, she sat down heavily in a chair, bringing the brandy to her lips and taking a gulp. The liquid sent fire all through her, but it did not bring any hope. Instead, she felt tears fill her eyes once more and, before she could stop herself, her shoulders trembled and sobs shook her frame.

Her affection for Lord Harlow meant nothing. His eagerness to court her would come to naught. It had all been torn from her, when she had only just been blessed enough to take a hold of it. And all because of her own foolishness. If only she had remained out of the way, had kept herself from rushing inside, then perhaps now she would be just as free as she had been before! But now it was all gone. Everything lay in pieces around her feet. All that lay in her future now was darkness.

CHAPTER FIVE

"You have been quiet this afternoon, Lady Christina."

Much to Richard's shock, Lady Christina barely glanced up at him but kept her face turned a little away from him as the carriage made its way through London, back to Lady Christina's home. Richard glanced towards Lady Newfield, who was, he noticed, sitting tight-lipped, her eyes blazing with some unspoken anger and her hands held tightly in her lap. Was it that he had done something wrong? Had he spoken foolishly on some matter or other? Had he displeased Lady Newfield in some way? Or upset Lady Christina? He could not think of what he had done, for whilst they had walked together, they had spoken of many things and none had seemed to bring her any dismay. She had not seemed quite herself, however, for her ready smile had not been present and her eyes had barely met his. And now, now that they were to return home, she appeared to have retreated into herself all the more. Richard's brow furrowed, his stomach tightening in knots as he looked back at Lady Christina, wondering how he could get her to speak to him.

"I do hope I have not upset you in some fashion," he said slowly, wondering if it would be best for him to speak plainly. "If I have, I pray that you would tell me, Lady Christina, so that I might rectify the situation at once."

Finally, she turned to him—but as she did so, Richard noticed that her eyes were swimming with tears and that there were dark smudges beneath them. His heart twisted in his chest, hating to see her in such distress. What was it that troubled her so?

"I am sorry, Lord Harlow," Lady Christina said, a little tightly, "but I can assure you that it is nothing that you have done that has brought me to this...state of mind." Her smile did not reach her eyes and barely lifted the corners of her mouth. "I do not mean to be so melancholy."

"But you are," he said gently, not meaning to make her feel in any way guilty but expressing concern. "What is it, Lady Christina? I would have you tell me, if only so that your burden might be a little eased."

She closed her eyes, and to his horror, a single tear slipped down onto her cheek. "You will hear soon enough, Lord Harlow," she said, in an ominous fashion. "And when you do, I pray that you will not hold it against me, for I swear to you that I have had no choice in the matter."

He blinked rapidly, looking from her to Lady

Newfield and back again. "You mean that you cannot tell me what troubles you?"

"No," she answered, her voice hoarse. "I cannot, for it would bring me too much pain and I fear that I would lose my composure entirely." Her eyes fastened to his for just a moment before she turned her head away again, looking out of the carriage window and evidently refusing to say another word. Richard did not know what to say or what to do, looking at the lady and finding himself completely at a loss as to how to help her. His mind filled with questions as he tried to work out what she could mean by what she had said, a sense of panic grasping his heart as his worst fears began to take hold of him. Was he not to have the happiness he had hoped for? Was he now to find himself alone, bereft of the young lady he had only just begun to court?

"I cannot tell you how much I have enjoyed this afternoon, Lord Harlow," Lady Christina said, her voice overly quiet and her eyes still fixed to the carriage window. "It has been one of the most wonderful afternoons of my life."

There was a note in her voice that made him feel as though she were saying farewell, as though she were stepping away from him. He did not know what to say, wanting to speak to her but unable to find the words. Seeing how Lady Newfield was steadily looking out of the *other* carriage window, Richard took a breath, reached across, and set his hand over Lady Christina's, making her turn her head as she inhaled sharply. He did not remove his hand from her own but let it linger, holding her gaze and waiting for her to say something. When she did not, he shook his head and closed his eyes, trying to find what he wanted to say.

"I have found this afternoon to be the culmination of all my hopes," he said softly. "To be in your company, Lady Christina, to spend time with you and you alone, is all that I should ever want."

This, unfortunately, did not bring any sort of happiness to Lady Christina's face. Rather, she pressed one hand to her mouth as tears spilled from her eyes. Richard began to panic, fearing that he had now made her sorrow all the worse, only for the carriage to draw up. Without even a word of farewell, Lady Christina practically jumped down to the pavement, hurrying up the stone stairs without a glance behind her.

Left within the carriage, Richard and Lady Newfield exchanged glances. Lady Newfield shook her head, a heavy sigh pulled from her lips.

"Please, do not make yourself anxious over your own behavior," Lady Newfield said quietly, her eyes searching as she looked back at him. "I can assure you, Lord Harlow, that this has nothing whatsoever to do with you. Although I can promise you that Lady Christina's grief and regret is quite genuine." Rising, she made her way to the edge of the carriage, looking over her shoulder at him. "Do not hold it against her, Lord Harlow. That is the only thing I will ask of you."

Richard nodded but said not a word, watching Lady Newfield as she walked up into the house. The footman closed the door, and Richard could only slump back against the squabs, pressing his fingers to his temples. The carriage rolled forward, the driver aware that he now needed to return home, but Richard took no notice. Why had Lady Christina appeared so upset? What was it that he was not to hold against her? As far as he was aware, they were to be courting now, and Lady Christina had been just as eager as he.

A sudden thought came to his mind, and he rapped on the roof.

"To Whites!" he shouted as the driver replied that he had heard him. Whites, whilst perhaps not overly busy at this time of day, would certainly have a few gentlemen within it, and surely someone there would know if anything particular had happened. Anything that involved Lady Christina, at least.

WHITES WAS QUIET, but there were a few patrons present at the very least. Muttering to a footman, Richard sat down quickly in a large, overstuffed chair and waited until his drink was brought to him. Taking it from the footman's tray, he sat back and let himself almost sink into it. His eyes roved about the room. There were a few others present, but some were dozing whilst others conversed quietly. He recognized a few but certainly none that he would ask about any sort of gossip! Sighing to himself, Richard rubbed one hand over his eyes before throwing back his whisky. This evening was to be a soiree at Lord Bannister's townhouse, but he had no eagerness to return home and prepare for it. All Richard wanted to do was find out who might know something that involved Lady Christina.

"That ridiculous baron is back in London," he heard someone say, but rolled his eyes to himself at such a trivial remark. "Have you heard of his exploits?"

"I do not think I wish to know what Baron Fulham has been doing," said the second gentleman with a snort, echoing Richard's sentiments exactly. "That man is nothing more than a fool."

"His son is in London," the first man remarked. "Just as ridiculous and as obnoxious as his father, I am sure."

I am certain of it, Richard agreed silently, taking a sip of his whisky. He did not know who the gentleman was who was speaking, but he felt quite certain the man was of sound character, given he thought so poorly of Baron Fulham!

"I heard he is now engaged," said the second man, sounding quite thoughtful. "Although who would accept the son of a baron, I cannot imagine!"

The first footman laughed. "Perhaps it is someone quite desperate," he said, chortling. "Someone who has a disgraced sister or daughter or the like. That must be it, for I cannot imagine that anyone with any sense would give their consent to such a gentleman as that!"

Richard felt a cold hand grasp his heart as he listened to the two gentlemen speak. For whatever reason, something the gentlemen had said sent a flurry of fear into his heart. Hearing that Baron Fulham's son was engaged rose like a great warning in his chest and, in his mind's eye, he saw the pale face and teary eyes of Lady Christina.

Surely it could not be!

Rising from his chair, he strode to his right and

towards the two gentlemen, stopping just for a moment to bow low.

"Pardon me for interrupting your conversation," he said hastily, not even bothering to greet them both nor attempt to make an introduction, "but I must know who the young lady is that is engaged to...to..." Realizing he did not know the name of the son, Richard gestured impatiently. "Engaged to Baron Fulham's heir."

The two gentlemen looked at each other before they returned their gaze to Richard.

"This is a little untoward, my good sir," said the first gentleman, "being interrupted in such a way."

"I apologize," Richard said quickly, "but I have need to know of the lady's name." He did not give any explanation as to why but looked back steadily at the two men, shifting his gaze from one to the other until, finally, the second gentleman spoke up.

"The heir is named the Honorable Stephen Markham," said the second man, watching Richard with a hard gaze. "And he is to wed the Earl of Enfield's daughter, Lady Christina."

Richard could not say a word, feeling the ground shift under his feet. That was why Lady Christina had been so quiet that afternoon, because it was to be the one and only time they were to court. The only time she was to step out with him, the only time she was to remain by his side and be entirely his. Now, it seemed, she was to wed another, and what was worse, wed to someone who was not at all the right sort of gentleman for her—as far as Richard was concerned, this "honorable Lord Markham" would not bring Lady Christina any sort of happiness, and from how she had behaved in the carriage, she would be deeply unhappy for the rest of her days.

"I cannot quite believe it," he found himself saying. "Are you quite certain?"

The two gentlemen stared at him.

"Yes," said the second fellow said, slowly. "It is as we have said. Her name is now attached to his."

"And when did this happen?" Richard asked, finding it harder and harder to speak without his voice breaking with emotion. "Surely it cannot have been recent."

The first gentleman shrugged. "Only this morning," he said, with a strange look in Richard's direction. "You are not the last to hear of it, however. I am sure it will be all over London by this evening, of course!"

He chuckled, but Richard did not join in. Instead, he turned on his heel and walked back to his seat, gesturing to the footman. Ordering another brandy, Richard sat down heavily and folded his arms across his chest as though that would help him appear settled and at ease. However, his mind was spinning, filled with upset, sorrow, and confusion. The lady he had been courting was now apparently betrothed to someone else. How could that be? He had never once heard of Lady Christina having any interest in the baron's son—Mr. Markham, or whatever his name was. And for the daughter of an earl to marry a man without title, who would, in time, only inherit a barony, was all the more unusual. What had happened to induce the Earl of Enfield to marry off his daughter to someone of such a low position as this?

"Your brandy, my lord."

Richard took the glass and threw back the brandy in two gulps. "Another," he grunted, looking steadfastly at the floor as he tried to place his thoughts in order. Part of him wanted to return directly to Lady Christina's house, to beg to see her and to then demand to know how such a thing had taken place and why, after such evident delight at accepting his courtship, had she now become betrothed to Mr. Markham? But then he recalled the tears in her eyes, the way she had begged him not to ask her any further, to allow her explanation to remain silent for fear that she would lose her composure, and his heart twisted painfully within him. If he did such a thing, then no doubt, Lady Christina would be even more upset than she was at present. It had been clear that she had been very distressed, which told Richard that she had not been a willing partner in this arrangement.

"I will have to meet this Mr. Markham," Richard growled, his hand curling into a tight fist. "I will see what it is about him that has made him so particular in the eyes of Lord Enfield." His jaw tightened as he considered what he was to do next. Was he going to give up, to give in now that Lady Christina had discovered herself engaged? It was, of course, the most sensible thing to do, for any gentleman who found that his particular lady was now betrothed to someone else would give up his pursuit immediately, believing himself to be quite lost to it now. However, Richard was not quite so willing. Given what he had only just discovered within his heart for the lady, he had no eagerness to turn his back on her and leave her to her marriage. Not when he knew that she was less than inclined towards her betrothed!

Will you elope with her?

It was an idea, Richard mused, considering what Lady Christina's response would be should he ask her to do so. Perhaps she would be glad of his willingness; perhaps she would be all the more eager to go with him so that she might escape Mr. Markham. Yes, an elopement might bring scandal and embarrassment with it, but he could still put it to Lady Christina and allow her to make her choice, surely?

"I will not give up," he told himself aloud, his voice thin. "No matter what the truth is, I shall not give up."

GOING to the soiree at Lord Bannister's was not something that Richard found any joy in, yet he knew that it was necessary for him to do so. He had accepted the invitation, and given he was not unwell, he could not be so rude as to remain at home. Despite the pain in his heart and the heaviness of his mind, Richard forced himself to dress and to make his way to Lord Bannister's for what would be, of course, an overly jolly evening. Lord Bannister was well known for providing all manner of entertainment, which most of the *ton* found to be utterly enchanting, but to Richard, would be nothing more than an evening to endure.

"You do not look as though you are enjoying your evening, Harlow."

The voice of Lord Prestwick was not the balm that Richard needed. "That is because I am not particularly enjoying it, Prestwick," he said, a little sharply. "Pray, do not come to fill my ears with all manner of nonsense. I am in no mood to hear it this evening."

This, he knew, was unfair of him to say, but the truth was, he did not want to hear a single word about Miss Allerton and whether or not Lord Prestwick still found her just as enchanting as he had done before.

"My goodness, you are a little ratty this evening," Lord Prestwick answered, but without any sort of malice in his voice. "I presume this is to do with Lady Christina?"

Richard rounded on him, his brows low and his eyes narrowed. "What do you mean?"

Lord Prestwick settled a hand on his arm, a gentleness in his eyes that Richard had not expected.

"You had come to care for her, I think," he said quietly. "And now the news is all around London that she is going to marry the heir to the Fulham barony."

Richard's heart ached anew as Lord Prestwick spoke. "I spoke to Lady Christina myself," he said, dropping his head, his anger fading away. "I know that she is not willing to marry this man, but, for whatever reason, she is being forced to do so."

Lord Prestwick spread his hands. "Is that not the way for many a young lady?" he asked with a shake of his head. "Perhaps that is something we ourselves can recall if we are ever blessed with daughters!"

Frustrated, Richard closed his eyes and took in a steadying breath. "I cannot betray myself to everyone here," he said in a low voice. "And yet the pain in my heart is greater than I think I can bear. I have been in Lady Christina's company for so long, and yet it has only been within the last sennight that I have found myself to be so firmly drawn towards her."

"Your heart is involved," Lord Prestwick said as he had done before. "And that is why the pain is now so great."

"I am determined not to give in," Richard told him firmly. "I must see Lady Christina again. I must speak to her. I must know what she is feeling and what she is fearful of. I must...give her the chance to escape."

Lord Prestwick's eyes widened. "You intend to offer to elope with her?"

Richard glanced about him before nodding. "It is as though I was in a darkened room and, in one single moment, the drapes were pulled back and I could see clearly," he said honestly. "I saw Lady Christina as the desire of my heart. And I do not intend to lose her now."

"Then I can only hope that you are successful," Lord Prestwick answered quietly. "I can tell that she means a great deal to you, but an engagement is very difficult to break, Harlow. Do take care." His eyes suddenly flared and, as Richard watched, Lord Prestwick frowned hard, his lips pulled tight and his shoulders a little hunched.

"I think you shall have to show a great deal of discretion, Harlow," he said as Richard slowly turned around, his eyes following in the direction of lord Prestwick's gaze. "You must control yourself at all costs, old boy. Now is not the time to lose your head."

Richard's heart stopped for a moment as he took in the object of his affection, and, alongside her, a gentleman that was short in stature and, from the way he held Lady Christina's arm in what was a possessive manner, clearly her betrothed. Richard had met the man once already, he realized, back at the night at Chadwick House, but he had paid the fellow very little attention. To see him now, standing by Lady Christina and with an arrogant smile on his face, made Richard's anger begin to burn furiously within him—especially when Lady Christina herself looked to be deeply upset. Her face was white, her eyes darting from one place to the next, and, as he watched, he saw her trying to gently tug her arm from Mr. Markham's.

Only for Mr. Markham to slap his free hand down over hers and lean in to say something to her.

"Steady," Lord Prestwick murmured, reaching to grasp Richard's arm in much the same manner. "You cannot go making a fool of yourself, Harlow. Mr. Markham may not even know of your affection for Lady Christina. Allow him to remain in such a position so that, should all go to plan as you hope, he will not know where to look for you, nor who might have taken her from him."

Lord Prestwick's words brought a shred of calmness to Richard's furious mind, and he took a step back, allowing Lord Prestwick's hand to drop from his arm.

"Speak to Lady Christina when you can," Lord Prestwick said calmly, "but do not do so in a manner that will draw attention to yourself. And ensure that her betrothed is far away when you do so."

"I do not think I can wait that long," Richard grated, as, finally Lady Christina looked up, her gaze suddenly meeting his. Her face paled, and she dropped her eyes to the floor, clearly either embarrassed or ashamed— although, he noted, her hand was now free of Mr.

Markham's grasp. How he wished she felt neither emotion, wished that she felt hope when she looked into his face! The urge to go to her at once, to pull her from Mr. Markham and to tell her that she had no need to feel any sort of shame, burned hot within him, but he forced himself to remain where he was.

"I will speak to her," he grated, half to himself. "Might you be able to distract Mr. Markham for a time, Prestwick?" He glanced at his friend, who was grimacing. "I know that he is not the most amiable of gentlemen, but I must have an opportunity to speak to Lady Christina."

This brought a look of understanding to Lord Prestwick's face. "Very well," he said quietly, his expression one of sympathy. "My goodness, man, you must feel a very great deal for Lady Christina indeed."

Richard closed his eyes as the words hit him hard. "I do," he said slowly. "I feel a great deal, indeed. In fact, I feel so much that I think I will do almost anything to ensure that she is removed from Mr. Markham's arm." His jaw worked furiously. "And the sooner it is done, the better."

CHAPTER SIX

There had been nothing for Christina to do other than to accept the situation without question. Her father had apologized countless times, but it did nothing to bring her any sort of relief. It had been made all the worse when Mr. Markham had appeared at the house, ready to call on her without having made any prior arrangement.

She had disliked him at the first. He was just as his father was, with such arrogance about him that it practically oozed from his every word and action. He had barely glanced at her but had made some remark about how he was delighted to be marrying the daughter of an earl, and had spoken at length about her dowry, wondering when he would receive it and seeking to know just how much it would be.

Both Christina and her father had remained utterly silent at this, overcome by the man's conceit and his clear disregard for either of them. When Mr. Markham had insisted that he would be taking Christina to the soiree this evening, Christina had tried to find some excuse, but Mr. Markham had not even looked at her. Rather, he had instructed her as to when she was to be ready and had taken his leave, with Christina and Lord Enfield staring after him with shock and dismay written over both their faces.

Once Mr. Markham had left, Lord Enfield had broken into yet more apologies, telling Christina that he was doing all he could to try to find a way to bring this engagement to an end, to find something to offer to Lord Fulham in her place, but in her heart, Christina had known that there was very little hope. The truth was, she did not want her father to fight a duel, for she knew all too well that he would die in an instant. It was better, she had told herself, to be wed to Mr. Markham and to have her father still living than to have herself free to marry Lord Harlow but to be without her father. As much as it pained her, she had to do her level best to keep her head held high and do what she could despite the fact she utterly despised her betrothed.

"Good evening, Lady Christina." Their host for the evening greeted her warmly, having already greeted Mr. Markham and Lady Newfield. "I am very glad you have been able to attend this evening." Lord Bannister smiled brightly at her, but Christina did not return it. She knew all too well that Lord Bannister would gain a high level of interest in his little soiree given her presence here this evening. No doubt, there would be many people talking about both herself and Mr. Markham, and Lord Bannister would receive many questions from others in society. Yes, it would bring him a good deal of attention also, but it was attention that Christina herself did not want.

"Thank you, Lord Bannister," she murmured before moving quickly away, ready to take the arm of Lady Newfield. She needed a little support, needed to have a little security, and Lady Newfield was the only one at present who could provide it.

"I think not."

Mr. Markham practically pushed Lady Newfield aside, stepping in front of her and offering her his arm. Christina recoiled inwardly but forced herself to take it, hating how he reached to pull her hand a little further through, so that she was almost pressed to his side. The possessiveness in this gesture made her stomach churn, and she turned her head away, seeing how Lady Newfield glared at Mr. Markham, her anger not at all hidden despite the company they were in at present.

"You will stay by my side," Mr. Markham said firmly, moving a little further forward into the room. "I will not allow you to remove yourself from me."

Christina stopped at once, refusing to walk any further. Mr. Markham's words were abhorrent to her, and she had absolutely no intention of allowing him to rule over her in such a dominant fashion.

"I do not think so," she said firmly, making to withdraw her hand. "I may be your betrothed, Mr. Markham —and might I remind you that I have had no choice in the matter—but that does not mean that you can force me to do as you please."

Before she could take her hand away completely, Mr. Markham reached across and grasped her wrist hard. His fingers pressed into her skin, and she had to bite her lip not to cry out.

"Do not be foolish, Lady Christina," he said, leaning towards her as though he wanted to whisper something lovely into her ear. "This is our first outing together as a betrothed couple, and *you* shall not make a fool of yourself or me."

Christina wanted to say something back to him, wanted to make some sort of retort, but found that she could say nothing. Her fear was still barreling through her, the pain in her wrist burning hot. To make things all the worse, when she turned her head away from Mr. Markham, her eyes found Lord Harlow looking at her, his gaze fixed and intense.

Shame rushed through her, recalling just how confused and upset he had been when she had spoken to him in the carriage. Her inability to tell him the truth, her confusing words and demeanor, had brought him no end of upset. She had seen it in his face—but had dared not tell him a word of truth for fear that something worse would happen to her father.

Dropping her eyes to the floor and aware that her face was burning hot, Christina wrenched her arm from Mr. Markham. There was something about seeing Lord Harlow, the only gentleman in her affections, that had given her a little more strength.

"What is it you think you are doing?" Mr. Markham hissed, his hand snaking out towards her—but before he could reach her, Lady Newfield swiftly stepped in between them both and slipped her hand through Christina's arm.

"It is as I have said, Mr. Markham," Christina answered, aware there was a slight tremor in her voice but refusing to allow her fear to conquer her. "I will not be ordered what to do and where to stand and who to speak to. I am my own person, and I shall continue on in such a fashion." She saw the fury in his face, the way his thick brows came low over his brown eyes, but steeled herself inwardly, still keeping her voice low. "And I do *not* expect you to ever grab my hand in such a manner again."

Lady Newfield pressed Christina's arm, a small smile on her face as she looked at Mr. Markham.

"Besides, Mr. Markham," she said as Christina let out a slow breath in an attempt to steady herself, "we would not wish to prevent you from conversing with the other gentlemen present whom, I am sure, will be very eager to hear exactly how you have managed to find yourself engaged to the daughter of an earl." There was a hint of ire in her voice, and Christina saw color begin to pour into Mr. Markham's face—but Lady Newfield did not wait any longer, begging Mr. Markham to excuse them both and then bodily turning Christina around so that they might walk away together.

"I think he is very angry, indeed," Christina whispered, praying that Lady Newfield would not take her in the direction of Lord Harlow. "But I thank you."

Lady Newfield smiled and urged Christina to a quieter part of the large room, gesturing to a footman to bring them both some refreshments as they came to a stop, hiding in the shadows just a little.

"You did very well yourself, Christina," Lady

Newfield said firmly. "I am astonished at the man's attitude towards you." She clicked her tongue, her disapproval more than apparent. "He may call himself a gentleman, but I am certain that he is not." Her eyes turned back to Christina, looking at her steadily. "How are you faring, my dear?"

The question seemed to unlock a flood of emotion that Christina had buried deep within her. Tears immediately sprang to her eyes, a shuddering breath shaking her frame, and she was forced to turn her head away so that she looked at the wall rather than at anyone else.

"I am sorry," Lady Newfield said gently. "Clearly, you are in deep distress."

"My father does not wish me to marry Mr. Markham," Christina said shakily. "I do not wish to either, and yet, there is no other choice." Closing her eyes, she forced the tears back. "I would not see him accepting a duel from Lord Fulham."

Lady Newfield shook her head as Christina opened her eyes, relieved that her vision was not particularly blurred with tears. "It is a very sorry affair," she said quietly. "Would that I could do something to help you, my dear. I will be honest and tell you that I have been thinking of nothing else since I discovered this news, but that, as yet, I have not come up with a solution."

"Nor I," Christina answered honestly, a rueful smile tugging at one side of her mouth. "But it is made all the worse given what I have had to be pulled away from."

Lady Newfield let out a long sigh. "And by that, you mean Lord Harlow," she said, her expression filled with understanding. "You must tell him the truth, Christina. I know that Lord Fulham has threatened consequences if you do not, but I do believe that you have nothing to fear in telling Lord Harlow what has occurred." Her shoulders lifted. "Mayhap, he will be just as willing as I to try to find a way out for you."

"I fear that I may have confused him too much," Christina answered, dropping her gaze. "I have seen him here already this evening, and the way he was looking at me..." She shook her head, unable to find the words to express just what she had felt when he had first caught her gaze.

"That does not mean that you should ignore him for the rest of the evening," Lady Newfield said gently. "I am sure that he would be glad to speak to you."

Christina took in a deep breath and dared to glance over her shoulder, wondering if she would be able to see Lord Harlow in the room, only, to her astonishment, to see him walking steadily towards her. In an instant, her heart tore into a panicked rhythm, afraid that Mr. Markham would see her speaking to Lord Harlow and that, somehow, he would know that he meant a great deal to her.

"Lady Newfield." Lord Harlow bowed quickly, before his eyes caught Christina's. "Lady Christina."

The way he said her name, with such tenderness and with such a kindness in his eyes, made her want to weep.

"Lord Harlow," she answered, bobbing a curtsy. "Good evening."

"Good evening."

He said nothing more, watching her carefully as she looked back at him. Her throat was tight, her chest constricting as she struggled to know what to say. The fact that he was not asking her anything only added to her distress, even though she knew that she was not meant to say anything about her present situation and how she had come by it.

"Lord Harlow."

Lady Newfield stepped in, obviously seeing Christina's distress.

"Lord Harlow, my dear niece has been placed in a very difficult situation," she said quietly. "It is not one that she is permitted to speak of, for there has been a threat against herself and her father should she do so."

Christina's eyes flared with alarm, and she put one hand out towards Lady Newfield, but her great-aunt merely caught her hand and pressed it tightly.

"She may not tell you, Lord Harlow, but I can," Lady Newfield continued as Christina's panic grew. "But only if you can assure us of your discretion. Of your promise not to engage yourself in this matter to the point that those already involved are aware of it."

There was an immediate objection on Christina's lips, but it died away the moment Lord Harlow surreptitiously reached across and pressed her other hand, reassurance in his eyes as he looked at her.

"You can be fully assured of it," he said, letting go of her hand quickly, although the brief touch meant a great deal to her. "You know very well that I have been worried about you, Lady Christina. I do want to know what has occurred, and why you have found yourself engaged to a man such as Mr. Markham!" His expression was one of complete confusion, and, although he kept his voice low, she could see just how agitated he was.

"Very well," she said, looking to Lady Newfield. "Pray, Lady Newfield, tell all to Lord Harlow, even though I am quite certain that it is all for naught." Her head dropped as Lady Newfield began to speak, unable to even look at Lord Harlow as he listened to the explanation. She did not know what he would think of her, fearing that he might consider her very foolish indeed for storming into her father's study in the way she had done. Mayhap, he might turn around and tell her that this situation was of her own making and that, had she not been so determined, so eager, then she might now find herself still courted by him. Had she not done so, she might have been able now to work with him to help her father. Her cheeks flared hot, her head dropping at little lower as her embarrassment grew. Any moment now, he would give her his sincere apologies that such a thing had happened but would, thereafter, step away.

"And that is the predicament Lady Christina now finds herself in," Lady Newfield finished. "A very difficult one indeed."

For a few moments, there was not a single response to Lady Newfield's explanation. Hot tears crept into Christina's eyes as she waited for him to reply, fearing now that he would turn away from her, leave her entirely alone and without hope.

"My goodness."

Lord Harlow's voice was grave.

"What a despicable creature Lord Fulham is."

Christina's head lifted at once, her eyes rounding as

she saw the anger flooding into Lord Harlow's face. "You do not think it my fault?" she asked, her voice tremulous, and Lord Harlow startled visibly as though what she had said had shocked him.

"How could I blame you?" he asked, his fingers once more finding hers, his gesture hidden by the shadows. "You have done nothing worthy of blame. Instead, you sought to protect your father in the only way you could. Indeed, Lady Christina, I admire your determination and your devotion to your father." He shook his head, releasing her fingers with obvious reluctance. "I am horrified to hear what Baron Fulham has done. I did not know anything about this situation, even though I was present that night. I was aware that there were some debts to be paid, but I certainly did not see your father writing any such vowel to Lord Fulham. If I had, I would have made certain to stop him."

Christina smiled tightly. "I believe that my father was a little in his cups," she said softly. "Not that I hold him responsible. No one could have expected Lord Fulham to have demanded such a thing from him."

"And if you do not continue with your betrothal, if you do not marry Mr. Markham, then your father will be forced into a duel, and you believe he will..." The sentence did not finish, and Christina nodded fervently, a single tear slipping from her eye.

"Then we must find a way to bring this entire situation to an end," Lord Harlow said with a firmness that astonished Christina. "Has a date been set?"

She shook her head. "Not as yet," she answered slowly. "I am not certain when such a thing might take place, for Mr. Markham seems to be, at present, reveling in what he has achieved.

Lord Harlow considered this carefully, his eyes dimmed with anger. "Then what can we do?"

Christina did not immediately answer, for such was the fervor in his voice and the determination in his eyes that she was quite overcome, having not expected anything of the sort from him. It took her a few moments to regain the power of speech, such was the joyful astonishment that captured every part of her.

"You must know, surely, that I wish to help you," Lord Harlow continued, looking into Christina's face and giving her a small, gentle smile. "I cannot have you marry this man, Lady Christina. He will only make the rest of your days miserable! He will not treat you with the respect and the consideration that you deserve. Even now, I observed him expecting you to be nothing more than a servant to his whims, doing as he asks without hesitation. Is that not so?"

Christina nodded, her throat aching. "It is."

"Then, of course, I shall assist you in this," he said softly. "I am sure that there will be a way for us to remove this particular difficulty from you." Drawing in a breath, he lifted his chin a notch. "I will not stand by and watch as you marry someone like that, not when there is more within my own heart for you than will ever be in his."

"Then how can I refuse you?" she whispered, her throat aching with the swell of relief that pressed down hard within her chest. "I do not want to marry Mr. Markham, Lord Harlow. The only gentleman I have ever considered in that regard is..." She closed her eyes, feeling the moment rising up around them, looking into his eyes and feeling the desire to say all that she wished and yet found so difficult to say.

"Then let us hope that this is what shall be," Lord Harlow said, clearly knowing what it was that she was trying to say and ensuring that she did not have to bring herself to say it when she was already deeply emotional. "For I will not rest until we have found a way to remove you from this, Lady Christina, until Lord Fulham is made fully aware that he cannot treat your father nor you in such a manner." His eyes glinted with steel, his jaw working hard for a moment. "I give you my promise, Lady Christina. You need not be in fear any longer."

CHAPTER SEVEN

The urge to go directly to Mr. Markham and to plant him a facer before demanding that he release Lady Christina from their betrothal had been very strong indeed—but Richard had resisted the urge with an effort. In fact, he had managed to be civil, making certain that he had found a way to be introduced to the fellow so that he might make a more thorough assessment of him.

He had not been mistaken in his first consideration of the fellow. Mr. Markham was smug, arrogant, and entirely ignorant of what it was to be a gentleman. Richard had been forced to endure watching Lady Christina standing next to Mr. Markham, a silent onlooker to her betrothed's conversations. Never once did Mr. Markham ask for her thoughts; never once did he attempt to draw her into their discussion. It was as though she meant nothing to him, as though he thought very little of her, whereas Richard knew that Lady Christina was a highly intelligent young lady who had much to contribute, should she be asked. To see her so ignored and belittled had made his fury burn all the hotter, but he had kept it buried deep within himself, not allowing Mr. Markham to see it. He had been nothing other than amiable so that Mr. Markham would not consider him to be any sort of threat.

However, this morning, Richard was determined to find a way to help Lady Christina out of her dilemma. Whilst Lady Christina did not hold her father responsible for what had occurred, Richard had to admit that there was a part of him that thought a little poorly of Lord Enfield. Had the man chosen not to drink so much liquor, then he might have kept his senses about him —although, Richard had to admit, there was never any single moment when he would have thought a gentleman to be as demanding and as cruel in his requests as Lord Fulham.

"Thank you for allowing me to call upon you so early," he said, sitting down in the drawing-room as Lord Prestwick sat down heavily in a chair, dark circles beneath his eyes. "I know it is most untoward, and yet I can assure you that it is of the greatest importance."

"It had better be," Lord Prestwick grumbled, shaking his head before pinching his nose and closing his eyes. "My tiredness is not at all satisfied as yet and last evening was a—"

"That is what I want to speak to you about," Richard interrupted. "Last evening, I met with Lady Christina."

Lord Prestwick's eyes flared as his attention piqued. "Lady Christina? I did see her speaking with you, of course. That must have been painful for you."

Richard waved one hand. "It was, but not for the reasons you might think," he said, before quickly expressing what Lady Newfield had told him. He saw Lord Prestwick's eyes flare, his mouth opening in astonishment, and hurriedly stated, quite firmly, that there was to be no mention of what he had just been told. "You must understand, should Lord Fulham or Mr. Markham become aware that this arrangement is known by either of us, then there may well be further consequences for Lord Enfield and his daughter."

Blinking rapidly, Lord Prestwick shook his head. "Indeed."

"Lord Fulham might demand a duel, for example," Richard finished. "Therefore, I am determined that this remain quiet but that, at the same time, we work together to try to help Lady Christina out of this situation."

"You wish her to marry you instead," Lord Prestwick noted without giving Richard a chance to argue. "I cannot blame you for that desire. It sounds like a terrible situation, and I have a deep sorrow for the lady in question—although what it is that you wish from me, I cannot yet understand." He looked at Richard questioningly. "And why, with such urgency, did you come to see me?"

"Because I am at a loss!" Richard exclaimed, throwing up his hands. "I have sworn to Lady Christina that I will not give up, that I will find a way to achieve success in this, and yet I cannot think of a single thing to do!" Raking his hands through his hair, he threw himself up from his chair. "I have been awake half the night trying to think of what to do, but as yet, I have had not a single helpful thought."

"And so you have come to me, the wisest of your

friends," Lord Prestwick said, his grin taking the edge from Richard's angst. "Is that not so?"

Richard closed his eyes, his hands dropping to his side. "I must think of something to do by which I can help her," he said heavily. "I cannot imagine her—cannot *allow* her to become his wife!"

Lord Prestwick's smile faded, and his brows knitted together. "It is a very difficult situation," he agreed quietly. "Lord Fulham is a blaggard and no mistake. If Lord Enfield *has* written this particular vowel, however, then what can be done? A debt must be paid."

"But surely you agree that such a request is not at all acceptable?" Richard said, throwing his hands up. "What sort of fellow demands the residence of a gentleman in exchange for a few coin? What sort of man asks for the daughter's hand in marriage, else it will be a duel and nothing less?" Closing his eyes, he shook his head. "I want so desperately to comfort her, and she is looking to me for hope, Prestwick. What can I do but find an answer for her?"

The frown remained on Lord Prestwick's face for some moments, although he did not say anything. Instead, he looked back at Richard steadily, his thoughts clearly rushing through his head as he tried to find something to suggest, something that would force Mr. Markham and his father to step away from what they had demanded.

"Well, what I can think of at the first is that you must understand Mr. Markham," Lord Prestwick said, slowly. "You must understand his weaknesses, just as you must understand Lord Fulham's weaknesses also."

"I do not want to go anywhere near those gentlemen!" Richard protested, but his friend waved a hand.

"How else are you going to find a way into this situation if you do not know what sort of gentlemen they are?" he asked, lifting one eyebrow. "Yes, we know they are callous, cruel, and entirely self-centered, but what if there is something that they seek that they might inadvertently give away? Something that they desire more than Lady Christina?"

Richard closed his eyes, wanting to protest but realizing he could not.

"Lady Christina must find as much courage as possible," Lord Prestwick continued firmly. "She must make herself as disagreeable and as difficult as she can, in the faint hope that Mr. Markham might be a little dissuaded from the match."

"I do not think that such behavior will achieve anything," he said with a heavy sigh. "Lord Fulham is desperate for his son to reach greater heights than he himself has managed. That is why he first wanted the Enfield estate—so that he might give the illusion that he was wealthy enough to rent such a magnificent property as well as soon owning the smaller estate of his father's." One shoulder lifted in a small, hopeless shrug. "Given Mr. Markham is now to wed the daughter of an earl and receive what is, I am sure, a magnificent dowry, he will have achieved a great deal more than Lord Fulham already, and I am sure will not want to give her up in any way, regardless of just how difficult she might appear."

Seemingly now a little irritated at Richard's determination to refuse every single suggestion, Lord Prestwick shook his head and pointed one finger out towards him.

"Regardless, she must try," he said firmly. "She will have to do as you ask in the hope that it may, perhaps, do something." He looked keenly at Richard. "Do you think you will be able to convince her?"

Richard hesitated. "I will have to take great care in how and when I see her," he said slowly. "Lord Fulham, I am sure, will be taking pains to ensure that she is doing as he has demanded, and, if I were to show particular interest in her, that would not bode well for either of us."

"Regardless, you must find a way," Lord Prestwick said with a shrug. "We also know that Lord Fulham is keen to play cards and to gamble." He looked at Richard pointedly. "Would it be too easy to suggest that we play him at cards and, thereafter, use what he has gained as a bargaining piece?"

Shaking his head, Richard pressed his lips hard together, his frown burrowing into his brow. "No, we cannot," he answered heavily. "Lord Fulham may win the game, and then what should we do?" He saw Lord Prestwick's shoulders slump. "And besides which, he might very well cheat if he is determined to win the game and not lose a single piece of what he has gained."

"Then we must continue on as planned," Lord Prestwick said with a determined gleam in his eye. "You shall continue your acquaintance with Mr. Markham; I shall continue my acquaintance with Baron Fulham—as much as I should not wish to." Grimacing, he sighed heavily. "But you must first find a way to go to Lady Christina. I know that she will wish to see you." Tilting his head, his eyes flared. "Could you not elope with her?"

Again, Richard shook his head. "If I do so, then her father might very well be called into a duel with Lord Fulham for breaking the terms of the agreement, even though it is not he who has done so," he said with a heavy sigh. "Otherwise, I would have taken her almost immediately to Scotland and might very well be wed by now." A half-smile caught his lips. "It is a good thought, however."

Lord Prestwick smiled ruefully. "I thank you for that." Briskly, he rose to his feet. "Now, you are to go to Lady Christina's, yes?"

"I cannot go at once, no," Richard answered slowly. "I shall write to her and suggest that, mayhap, we accidentally meet at the very same bookshop we met at a short time ago. That way, if anyone is watching her, they will think nothing of her entering a bookshop with Lady Newfield. It will be just as normal."

"A wise thought," Lord Prestwick agreed, making his way across the room and ringing the bell. "And before then, perhaps something to eat?" His grin reappeared. "You may have had something to refresh yourself this morning, but I certainly have not, given I was so *rudely* awakened by your presence."

"Perhaps I could have a little something," Richard agreed, feeling a trifle more relieved now that he had spoken to Lord Prestwick and unburdened himself a little. "Might I also write to Lady Christina?"

Lord Prestwick nodded. "But of course," he said. "And I shall have my man take it there directly the moment you are finished. Would that please you?"

"Thank you," Richard replied honestly. "You are a true friend, Prestwick, and I truly appreciate your assistance."

~

STEPPING into the bookshop brought with it a swell of memories. This had been the bookshop where he had first seen Lady Christina in a new way, when he had felt a sting of jealousy that she had not looked at him but at Lord Prestwick. A small smile played about his mouth as he walked a little further inside. This place, if anything, gave him a little more hope.

He was the first one to arrive, although there were a few other visitors within the shop also. Lord Prestwick had not joined him, thinking it best to remain away from Richard when he met with Lady Christina. Thus, Richard was entirely alone, and his anticipation in seeing Lady Christina was growing steadily. Even though he did not have any plan as yet, even though he had not any hope to offer her, the eagerness to see her was all the more apparent.

Wandering through the bookshop, Richard allowed himself to recall all that he had felt the day he had first seen Lady Christina in an entirely different light. It had been grown to such overwhelming heights that he had soon found himself entirely encompassed, feeling now the deep affection that had been within himself for so long but never before truly revealed.

She had been a little melancholy that day, he remembered, recalling the urge to make her smile. When she had done so, he had felt his heart lift and had felt himself glad that she no longer had a sorrowful expression about her. How he hoped that he might be able to do the very same now! At the very least, he could reassure her that he and Lord Prestwick were working together to come up with an idea that would release her from her bond.

Hearing the chime of the bookshop bell as the door opened, Richard turned around at once, his eyes meeting those of Lady Christina's almost. He made to rush towards her only for Lady Newfield to take her great-niece's arm in her own and to lead her away from where Richard stood.

Immediately realizing what Lady Newfield meant by such an action, Richard turned on his heel and made his way back to the books he had been absently perusing only a few moments before. Lady Newfield clearly did not want them to be too apparent, given that rumors spread all too quickly and all too easily through London society. Even in a bookshop, one could never be too careful!

Picking up a book and making some attempt to look at it, Richard kept his gaze firmly fixed on it for what felt like an eternity, whereas in reality, he knew it was probably only a few minutes. Looking up, he set the book down with a sigh and then made his way slowly to where he knew Lady Newfield and Lady Christina had gone. Taking meandering steps and making sure to fix his eyes on the books rather than on the ladies themselves, he feigned surprise when he came upon them both, even though his heart was practically screaming with the joy of being back by her side again.

"Good afternoon, Lady Newfield, Lady Christina," he said, keeping his voice low so as not to disturb the others in the bookshop. "How very good to see you."

Lady Christina tried to smile, but it was rather wane, her cheeks pale and her eyes a little dim.

"Good afternoon," she replied quietly as Lady Newfield took a small step back, letting him speak directly to the lady. "It is good to see you, Lord Harlow."

There was a hope in her eyes that she could not hide, hope that he was reluctant to quench. "After last evening, you cannot know how relieved my heart was, how glad I was to hear you speak such kind words."

"I have been thinking of what I can do to assist," he told her, seeing how her eyes flared for just a moment. "I will also tell you that Lord Prestwick is also aware of this situation now, but solely so that I can have someone else to speak to, to come up with ideas and the like." Aware of the alarm in her expression, of the whiteness that had pulled the color from her cheeks, Richard tried to quickly reassure her. "He has the utmost discretion, Lady Christina, and I am sure will be of benefit to us both."

Letting out a slow breath, Lady Christina tried to smile, but her lips barely curved. "I see," she said softly. "If you vouch for him, Lord Harlow, then I will, of course, trust your judgment." Her voice still quiet for fear of disturbing the bookshop, she continued to speak. "I know it is very soon after we have spoken, but have you had any thoughts as to what we might do?"

Richard hesitated and, as he took a breath, he saw the brightness fade in Lady Christina's eyes. The frustration settled within him like a tightly knotted ball, but he forced himself to speak honestly.

"Lord Prestwick is to befriend Lord Fulham, and I shall continue my acquaintance with Mr. Markham."

Lady Christina's expression changed to one of utter horror. "But why should you wish to do such a thing?" she asked, her voice rising just a little. "Surely to make him further acquainted with you will, in fact, only make his awareness of you, and perhaps your intentions, all the more apparent?"

"I do not think so," he said gently, reaching out to take her hand and squeezing it. "In fact, I think it will have the very opposite effect. We will, of course, have to make sure that Mr. Markham does not see us in conversation very often, but I am certain that, otherwise, he will not have any reason to suspect anything untoward."

Her hand shifted in his, her fingers lacing through his own, and immediately, Richard felt heat spiral up. How desperately he wanted to take her in his arms! How eager his heart was to claim her as his own, and yet, he could do nothing of the sort.

"And what shall I do?" she asked, a small flicker of determination growing in her eyes as she looked back at him. "There must be something I can do to further things myself?"

"Indeed," he said, encouraged by the lift of her chin and the way her trust in him had now led her towards finding courage within herself. "You must attempt to make yourself quite out of favor with him. In fact, you must make yourself quite dislikable in every way so that he is not at all inclined towards you." Seeing how her mouth opened and fully aware that there would be a protest upon her lips, he stepped a little closer to her and smiled into her eyes.

"I am aware that you are, in fact, the grand prize to Mr. Markham and that, in marrying you, he will improve his standing in society as well as gain a very large dowry from your father. Therefore, you believe that no matter how much you might wish to behave in such a way, it will make no difference to him."

"That is it precisely," she agreed, her face gaining a little color as she looked up at him.

"But nevertheless, you must find the courage to do so," he told her. "It may come to naught, but, at the very least, it will prove to him that you are not to be so easily trifled with."

Lady Christina bit her lip, her eyes doubtful. "I am afraid of what he will do to me if I do not behave as he expects," she told him quietly. "Last evening, he was very angry with me, indeed."

"But I shall be with you," Lady Newfield reminded her great-niece, speaking from where she stood. "He will not lay a hand on you, my dear. Your father and I shall make quite certain of it."

Trying to encourage her further, Richard smiled into Lady Christina's anxious expression, suppressing his anger that had exploded within him at the mention of Mr. Markham's cruel nature. "And I am sure that, within a few days, I shall have something to put into action," he said firmly, with a good deal more confidence than he had ever felt before this moment. "You will be free, Lady Christina."

Lady Christina dropped her gaze to the floor, and immediately, Richard's stomach sank with a sense of dread. What was it that Lady Christina feared?

"We may have less time than I might have first thought," she said softly. "I believe that I told you yesterday that Mr. Markham did not intend to set our marriage date for some time yet." Her eyes lifted to his and then dropped again. "I fear I was mistaken in my judgment."

Richard's heart seemed to stop for a moment, and he lowered his head just a little, his mouth dry as deep anxiety caught hold of him.

"He has set a date, it seems," Lady Christina continued, her cheeks losing their color as she looked up at him. "It is for three weeks hence."

"Three weeks?" Richard repeated, his voice drilling very low indeed. "But it is less than a month until—"

"It is, yes," she answered quietly. "The final set of banns will be called on the very day of our marriage, it seems." Her hand loosened in his, her head bowing low. "Everything is being arranged as Mr. Markham wishes it. I do not know what is happening."

"Then you must try to discover it," he told her, trying to be as direct and yet as gentle as possible. "And I swear to you, Lady Christina, if the worst should happen and we cannot find a way to free you and to protect your father, then I shall elope with you and take your father with us if I have to!" Reaching out, he felt her hand touch his, her finger tentative but finally, and with great joy in his heart, saw her smile. "I shall deal with the consequences thereafter."

"I care very deeply for you, Lord Harlow," Lady Christina whispered, her words meant only for him. "I wish I had been bold enough to tell you so before. Then perhaps now, these dreadful circumstances might not be upon us."

Her words lifted his spirits more than he could express. His fingers tightened on hers and, before he could prevent himself, before he could glance around to ensure no one saw him, his other hand was at her cheek, his fingers brushing down over her warm skin as her lips curved with a renewed hope.

"Let us look to the future with certainty in spite of our circumstances," he said softly, making her smile blossom all the more. "No matter what we may face, I believe that we shall achieve our happiness, Lady Christina. In fact, I am quite determined that we shall do so."

CHAPTER EIGHT

"You must now feel a little more hope, surely."

Christina looked at herself in the mirror and took in her pale cheeks, the dark circles beneath her eyes, and sadness that seemed to linger in her expression.

"It was a reminder of what I have to lose," she answered honestly. "But I do trust Lord Harlow. If he states that he will make certain I am removed from Mr. Markham before the wedding date, then I shall believe him."

Lady Newfield looked on approvingly. "Excellent," she said briskly. "You must not lose heart. Although, I did hear what Lord Harlow asked of you." Her eyes slid back towards Christina's reflection as the maid finished dressing her hair. "Do you think you can do as he asks?"

Christina took in a breath. "I can," she said, despite the quaking in her heart. "I can be disagreeable, I am sure, although I am not convinced that my behavior will make any difference whatsoever."

"Then we shall have to wait and see," Lady Newfield

answered with a small smile. "Come now. The carriage—and your father—will be waiting."

WALKING into Lord Fulham's townhouse and thereafter, into his drawing-room, Christina made certain to look all about her in what she hoped was an unimpressed air. It was to no avail, however, for one quick look at Mr. Markham, and Christina knew he had not given her the slightest notice. He was, in fact, looking away from her with a smug smile on his face as though he knew precisely how awful she was feeling and was glad of it. It was almost enough for Christina to give up but feeling the touch of Lady Newfield's hand on her arm reminded her that she was not to be pushed back so easily. She had stood up to Mr. Markham once already and, given what Lord Harlow had asked of her, she would continue to do so again.

"Good evening, Lady Christina."

Christina kept her face turned away from her betrothed, ignoring him as best she could. "Good evening," she murmured out of the side of her mouth.

"You had better teach your daughter how to address her husband to be, Lord Enfield!" Lord Fulham boomed, his voice so loud it seemed to rattle the candlesticks on the mantlepiece. "That is sheer insolence!"

Lord Enfield said nothing but took a small step towards Christina. She looked up at him, wondering whether or not he would berate her, but instead saw a small glint of steel in his eyes.

"And why did you *insist* on bringing the great-aunt?" Lord Fulham continued as Lady Newfield drew herself up to her full height. "Foolishness, a girl like that needing a great-aunt to care for her."

"I think you will find that it is I who have requested to be in Lady Christina's company," Lady Newfield said sharply. "Now, is that the dinner gong?"

Christina dared a smile at Lady Newfield as Lord Fulham turned puce as he glared at Lady Newfield. If anyone could show her what it meant to have courage, to have determination and strength, then Lady Newfield could do so.

"No, it was not," Lord Fulham muttered, throwing himself down into a chair. "Besides which, I have invited one or two other guests this evening. Simply so that we might have something to discuss since I am certain that there will be very little conversation from the three of you."

Balking at the sheer disdain and vulgarity that came from Lord Fulham's lips, Christina turned herself away from the man, meandering across the room so that she might look out of the window—although there was not a good deal to see, given the hour. She was being very rude, indeed, she knew, for she ought to be sitting next to her husband-to-be and, at the very least, being near to him even though she did not need to converse. By removing herself as far from him as she could, Christina knew that she was not creating a good impression.

She tried her best not to care, nor to fear what Mr. Markham would do in retaliation. Lady Newfield came to join her, as Lord Enfield sat down heavily in a chair and said nothing, the chair squeaking just a little under his weight.

"You are doing very well, indeed, especially in the face of such rudeness!" she said, her voice getting louder so that the end of the sentence could be heard more clearly. "Maintain it through the dinner and you shall be doing very well, indeed."

THE DINNER WAS, however, a dull affair. The gentlemen spoke loudly and at length—all save for Christina's father —whilst the ladies did nothing more than eat and then sit quietly until the next course was served. Lady Gilchrist, who had come to join them with her husband, seemed to be a mousey creature who had no eagerness to even speak a word to either herself or Lady Newfield, sat without expression, her eyes dull and her complexion almost gray. In her mind's eye, Christina saw herself as she might be in a few years, should she marry Mr. Markham—and the thought made her shudder.

"I think," Lord Fulham said, waving a hand and grinning in a delighted fashion at the ladies, "that it is time for the port."

Christina looked away from him at once, seeing the man was already half-drunk. A glance at Mr. Markham told her that he was much the same, for his eyes were half-closed and a ridiculous smile played about his mouth. He was propping his head up on one hand, his elbow on the table in what was a state of appalling social etiquette.

"The port!" Lord Gilchrist exclaimed, banging one

fist on the table as Lady Gilchrist rose quickly. "Yes! At once!"

"I think that we must depart," Lady Newfield said, leaning towards Christina. "Hopefully, we will be able to leave Lord Fulham's townhouse entirely soon, but for the moment, we must take tea."

"I can do that," Christina replied, rising gracefully and making her way towards the door. She ignored the lewd remark that came from Mr. Markham, even though it made her face go hot with embarrassment. Being the last lady to leave, Christina could not help but notice when another voice was heard from along the hallway, although she knew she ought not to listen.

Hesitating, Christina slowed her steps, seeing Lady Newfield look back over her shoulder and then begin to stop. Shaking her head no, so that Lady Gilchrist would not wonder where they had both gone, Christina waved a hand for her great-aunt to continue before walking softly back along the hallway, stopping for a moment as she reached the corner.

Yes, indeed. Someone *was* speaking and in anxious tones also.

"I must see him," she heard a man's voice say. "And I must see him at once."

"Mr. Markham is dining at present," came the reply of what Christina presumed was the butler. "He cannot be disturbed."

"He will be disturbed if he does *not* come to speak to me at once," came the now angry reply. "Tell him that Lord Sturrock wishes to see him at once. Else things will go badly for him."

Everything within Christina told her to hurry along after the ladies, to do as she was expected and to wait until the gentlemen had arrived. But then the words of Lord Harlow came to mind, and she forced herself to remain where she was, wondering what might occur should she do so. If she stayed hidden, if the butler was to fetch Mr. Markham, then surely it would be wise for her to linger, to hear what was said?

But there is always the chance of you being discovered, said a small voice in her head. *And what then?*

There was no time for her to consider things further, for the murmur of the butler told her that he had agreed and was now on his way to fetch his master. Her stomach tight with anxiety, Christina looked all around her and then, not sure what else she should do, hurried in the direction where she had last seen Lady Newfield.

She did not have to look for long. A small parlor was to her left, and Lady Newfield was already sitting down opposite Lady Gilchrist, who, Christina noted, did not have even the smallest flicker of interest in her eyes.

"You must excuse me," Christina said hastily, coming a little further into the room so that she might see Lady Newfield. "I believe I lost you both for a moment, for I was quite taken up with a painting on the wall." She smiled at Lady Gilchrist, but the lady simply looked back at her without speaking. It was, in a way, unnerving.

"I must beg you to excuse me again," Christina said quickly, taking in a deep breath and praying that her courage would not fail her. "I must excuse myself for a short time."

There was no other explanation needed, for ladies

often excused themselves so that they might find the powder room or other small room set aside for that specific use. Lady Gilchrist let out a long breath and looked away as though she was already tired of Christina's conversation, whilst Lady Newfield, wearing a look of concern on her face, merely nodded.

Christina stepped back out of the room again, her feet making barely any sound on the carpet. To her relief, she heard Mr. Markham's voice from a little further away, the sound echoing back to her. She stayed in place for a moment, not taking another step and straining hard to hear what was being said.

"Why did you come here?"

She closed her eyes and let out a slow breath before opening them and scurrying forward, her hands curling into tight fists as though that might help her keep control of herself. Now was not the moment to lose her nerve, even though she knew Lord Fulham might appear from the dining room and catch her walking past the door at any moment. Making her way past it carefully, Christina came to the place she had been standing only a few minutes before and chose to remain there again. Mr. Markham's penchant for liquor had, it seemed, made him a little less cautious than he ought to have been, for his voice carried clearly towards her, and he had not apparently thought about taking his unexpected guest to either the study or the library so that they might discuss matters in private.

"You have not been paying me your dues."

Christina's mind whirled as she blinked rapidly,

trying to understand what was being said. Mr. Markham was in debt?

"You know very well I cannot make such payments to you at present," Mr. Markham replied with an earnestness that surprised her. "But I shall, very soon. My betrothal agreement includes Lady Christina's dowry, which will be more than enough to pay my father's debts."

Christina's eyes flared wide with astonishment. Mr. Markham was somehow responsible for paying off the debts of his father? She had never heard something so astonishing before. Why was Lord Fulham not doing all he could to remove himself without the need to garner the help of his son?

"I do not care a jot about your betrothal, the dowry, or anything to do with your present state of happiness," came the hissed reply. "The money must be repaid. I am —I am in need of it."

For a moment, nothing more was said. And then, as Christina listened hard, her back pressed against the wall, she heard the small catch in Mr. Markham's voice as he spoke.

"I am doing what I can," he said with an evident attempt at firmness. "Why do you think that my father has gone to such lengths as this?" The slight slurring of his words was yet another indication that Mr. Markham was already in his cups, and thus, speaking with a freedom that she had not expected of him. Burying her face in her hands, Christina took in a deep breath, tugging the air through her fingers and allowing it to blow away. There was clearly more to the relationship between Lord Fulham and Mr. Markham than she had first thought, and, from what it seemed, Mr. Markham was doing what his father wished him to rather than what he desired.

"I will instruct my solicitors tomorrow," Christina heard Mr. Markham say. "Now, do not call on me again in such a fashion. Return to your home and to your pretty little wife and leave me to my own affairs."

For a few moments, nothing was said, and Christina wondered if it was the end of the discussion. And then, she heard footsteps returning to her and, in her haste, turned hurriedly and slipped. She went down on her hands and knees, scrambling up straight away, her feet caught in her voluminous skirts. Breathless, embarrassed, and afraid, she made her way to the small parlor and quickly sat down, praying that Lady Gilchrist did not notice her red cheeks.

"Tea, Lady Christina?" Lady Newfield asked, a look of uncertainty etched into her features as Christina nodded. "You were able to find us again, I see?"

"I was," Christina answered, smiling at the maid as she served the tea. "It was not far." She looked from Lady Gilchrist to Lady Newfield and tried to keep her conversation light. "My aunt tells me that you are a great reader, Lady Gilchrist."

It was a foolish remark, certainly, but it seemed to pull the lady from her doldrums. For the first time that evening, a flicker of a smile danced about her lips, and she looked more than a little pleased.

"I do enjoy reading," Lady Gilchrist replied in a soft, quiet little voice, but with such a broad smile that

Christina felt as though she had given her some sort of wonderful gift. "But there is always so much to read, of course." She threw up one hand as though this was the most irritating thing of all. "I shall never make my way through my husband's library."

Christina was about to state that she had not seen Mr. Markham's library, nor that of Lord Fulham, but instead of stating something like that, she merely kept her eyes lowered and tried to keep her breathing steady. When the gentlemen reappeared, she was afraid that her guilt might be easily read on her face, that she might find Mr. Markham staring at her as if he could tell what she had done. Lady Newfield rose from her chair, picked up a china cup filled with tea, and handed it to Christina, who took it with only a slight tremble in her hand. Her eyes met Lady Newfield and she smiled quickly, praying that her great-aunt- would not try to say anything—even something surreptitious—in front of Lady Gilchrist.

"I am sure Lady Christina enjoys reading also," Lady Newfield said, turning back to Lady Gilchrist. "As do I, I confess. I have not had much opportunity during the Season, however, for I—"

She was interrupted by the sound of a loud, uproarious laugh that seemed to snake into the room. As Christina turned her head, her tea still held in her hand, she saw her father, then Mr. Markham, Lord Gilchrist, and Lord Fulham, all make their way into the room.

The only one not swaying and stumbling was her father. Instead, his dull eyes caught hers, his brow furrowed. It was clear that he was having a very difficult time, indeed.

Christina swallowed hard, clenching her fists in her lap. She had overheard something she ought not to have, and, at that moment, had felt both fear and a sense of triumph. There was something now that Lord Harlow needed to hear, something that she could tell him that they should look into a little further. And yet to remain, when he might be able to tell by her face that she was feeling somewhat guilty, was too much of a difficulty to bear. Might she be brave enough to demand that they remove themselves from this situation? Could she be as rude and as inappropriate as would now be required?

Without any warning, Christina found herself standing tall, her feet placed flat on the floor, and a strength in her limbs that she not anticipated.

"I think we must take our leave, Lord Fulham," she said, her voice shaking a little but her determination steady. "My father is fatigued and, I am afraid, I have something of a headache."

Lord Fulham's easy smile faded at once and he looked at her with narrowed eyes, even though his gait was still a little unsteady.

"You cannot leave now," he said, dismissing her with a curtness that bit at her hard. "There is still an evening of entertainment!" He turned and made his way to a chair, sitting down heavily into it. "Sit, Lady Christina."

There was no discussion there, no suggestion that she would be able to wheedle her way out of this particular situation. Instead, Lord Fulham continued to talk to Lord Gilchrist, whilst Mr. Markham—whose demeanor now appeared to be brooding, given the darkness about his features and the way his eyes drifted about the floor rather than fix on anything—ignored her completely.

Christina drew in a deep breath.

"Father, shall we depart?" she said, walking towards her father, who had not yet sat down. "I have a headache and must retire to bed, and I can tell that you are fatigued." Seeing the frown pulling his brows low, she gave him a small yet terse nod, praying that he would not give in and that he would, in fact, be able to understand her eagerness to depart.

"But of course, we must depart if you are unwell," came the caring voice of Lady Newfield. "Our host will understand." She did not so much as glance at Lord Fulham, whose conversation with Lord Gilchrist had now faded to nothing. "Thank you for this evening, Lord Fulham."

Christina bobbed a curtsy. "I thank you," she said reluctantly before taking her father's arm and almost forcibly walking him to the door. Nothing was said, nothing was called out after them as they walked away, leaving Christina feeling all the more emboldened.

"That was very improper, Christina," her father chided, although the heaviness of his steps betrayed his despair and frustration. "I am certain that you do not truly have a headache, as you described to Lord Fulham."

A little indignant at her father's gentle correction, Christina looked up at him. "I will not pretend to enjoy my betrothed's company, Father," she said with more fervor in her voice than she had intended. "If I must make an excuse to remove myself from him, then so be it. I carry no guilt for doing so."

Lord Enfield sighed heavily, then stopped walking. Turning to her, he gave her a small, sad smile and nodded. "I should not have chided you so," he said, his voice low. "Forgive me, my dear."

"There is nothing to forgive, Father," she answered gently. "Come now. Let us go home."

CHAPTER NINE

Having to walk into a room and immediately attempt to discover the whereabouts of Mr. Markham was not something that Richard appreciated, but he did so, nonetheless. The evening gathering at Lord Pritchard's had been long planned, but thanks to some general conversation by Lord Prestwick, they had managed to discover that Baron Pritchard had, in fact, invited both Baron Fulham and Mr. Markham to his evening gathering. It was, therefore, with a little more intent that Richard stepped into the room, keeping his eyes sharp and his chin lifted high.

"Careful," Lord Prestwick murmured. "You are meant to be friendly and amiable, rather than angry and frustrated!"

Quickly rearranging his expression, Richard took a deep breath and tried to smile, reaching out to take a glass of brandy from a silver tray. "I feel like calling the gentleman out," he said darkly as Lord Prestwick picked up a glass also. "But instead, I must act as though I am his very dear friend."

"But look," Lord Prestwick murmured, his eyes bright as he turned his gaze from Richard to the door. "Lady Christina has only just arrived."

Every dark thought left Richard's mind at once. He turned quickly to look, his eyes fastening onto the figure of Lady Christina, who had entered along with Lady Newfield. Of Lord Enfield, there was no sign.

"Patience," he muttered to himself, knowing full well that he could not give into the urge to rush to her, to do as he had done before Mr. Markham and make his attention more than a little apparent. Instead, he was forced to watch Mr. Markham do what he himself desired to do, seeing the man sweep towards Lady Christina, bowing once and then taking her arm in a most possessive manner.

"Arrogant oaf," Richard muttered, as Lord Prestwick sighed and looked gloomily at him.

"I suppose I must do my duty," Lord Prestwick muttered. "I should greet Lord Fulham and make myself as amiable as possible."

"And I should do the very same to Mr. Markham," Richard replied begrudgingly. Setting his shoulders, he meandered slowly across the room in the vague direction of Mr. Markham.

Thankfully, the gentleman greeted him first.

"Good evening, Lord Harlow," Mr. Markham said, inclining his head and puffing his chest out in an important manner. "Are you acquainted with my betrothed, Lady Christina?"

Richard bowed, ignoring the way a cold hand tightened on his heart. "I am," he said slowly. "Good evening, Lady Christina."

She did not look at him, her eyes remaining downcast as she curtsied. "Good evening, Lord Harlow."

Mr. Markham cleared his throat, his chin still lifted and an arrogant smile flickering across his lips. "You will *have* to come to our engagement ball, Lord Harlow. It is sure to be a wonderful evening."

"How very kind," Richard responded quickly before another response could take hold of his tongue. "I would be delighted, of course."

"Might I ask," Lady Christina interrupted, her voice clear, and her eyes now fixed to Richard's, "whether or not I am to be informed as to when this ball is to take place, Markham?" Her gaze slid towards Mr. Markham, her hand slowly being pulled from his arm as she spoke— and Richard felt a swell of pride grow in his heart at her courage.

"You will know in due time," Mr. Markham replied tersely, a muscle tightening in his cheek as he glared at Lady Christina. "I am taking control of the details, of course. There is no need for you to be—"

"It is only because I have many friends that I should wish to invite," Lady Christina interrupted, and there was something in her voice that made Richard pay even greater attention. "For example, I should like to invite Lady Julia, Lord and Lady Greyson, as well as Lord Sturrock and Miss Marlow. Therefore, I should be given a little consideration when it comes to such invitations."

Richard's frown flickered over his brow, but Lady

Christina instantly looked towards Mr. Markham. His frown now firmly fixed, Richard slid his attention back towards Mr. Markham and was astonished to see that the gentleman had gone pale. No longer did he have that arrogant lift of his chin, or the small sneer tugging at his lips. Instead, he was staring at Lady Christina with such wide eyes that Richard was quite certain the gentleman had not expected her to mention either one—or more—of these names.

How very interesting, he thought to himself, his frown lifting slightly as he saw the triumphant gleam in Lady Christina's eyes. *Evidently, she has discovered something of note.*

"I do not think that you need invite anyone, Lady Christina," Mr. Markham said eventually, clearing his throat gruffly after he spoke. Giving himself a small shake as though this was all he needed to pull himself from this strange mood, he turned on his heel and walked away from them both, leaving Lady Christina and Richard standing together—without any sort of explanation.

"My goodness," Richard breathed, watching Mr. Markham walk away. "Whatever did you do, Lady Christina?" Turning back to look at her, he was delighted to see the broad smile on her face, the glee in her eyes, and the obvious happiness that came with what had just occurred.

"Last evening," Lady Christina began, "I overheard something. A gentleman named Lord Sturrock demanded to see Mr. Markham, even though the gentlemen were still at their port." She tilted her head just a little, still smiling at him. "I was on my way to the parlor to take tea with the other ladies when I thought to listen to what was being said."

"That was very courageous of you," Richard told her, feeling such a sense of anticipation rising within him that he was sure Lady Christina could feel it emanating from him. "What did you overhear?"

Quickly, Lady Christina told him, keeping her voice low. "This gentleman, Lord Sturrock, demanded that Mr. Markham pay his debts. Mr. Markham apologized and said he could not—he was speaking a little too openly given he had been drinking a good deal of liquor—but that he would use my dowry to pay for..." she looked all about her as though afraid someone would overhear her. "To pay for his father's debts."

Richard gaped at her for a moment before collecting himself and trying to regain some semblance of normality in his composure.

"I was astonished also," she told him, a small smile still playing about her mouth. "Why should Mr. Markham be paying for the debts of his father? Surely Lord Fulham is the one responsible for such things?"

"I would have thought so, yes," Richard answered slowly, his mind now whirling with a good many thoughts he could not put into order. "That is very strange. Very strange, indeed."

Lady Christina nodded. "And his countenance changed quickly when I mentioned Lord Sturrock's name, did it not?"

"It was very obvious, indeed," Richard agreed. "Pray, tell me—are you acquainted with Lord Sturrock? I have been introduced to him only the once."

Shaking her head, a look of doubt came into Lady Christina's eyes. "You do not think that he will be inclined to speak to Lord Sturrock to confirm the acquaintance?"

"No, I do not think so, although he certainly will not tolerate you speaking of the gentleman again," Richard answered. "I will have to speak to Lord Sturrock myself, Lady Christina—if you are contented to allow me to do so?"

Nodding, the worry faded from her eyes. "More than willing, Lord Harlow. I cannot tell you how relieved I am to have been able to share this with you—and for you to see just how upset it made Mr. Markham to hear that name mentioned!"

"It was very well done," he told her, seeing the way she practically beamed at him. "How do you fare yourself, Lady Christina?"

Her smile became gentle. "I am a little improved, now that I have some hope," she answered as Richard saw Mr. Markham begin to make his way back towards her. "It is good to see you, Lord Harlow."

"And for my eyes to see you," he told her, bowing low just as Mr. Markham reached them again. The color had returned to his cheeks, and he no longer appeared to be as upset as he had been before. Placing his hands behind his back, he cleared his throat to garner Richard's attention.

"Pray excuse my sudden departure," he said, by way of explanation. "I thought my father was signaling for my immediate attention, but I was mistaken. Entirely so."

"But of course," Richard said with what he hoped was a good measure of understanding in his expression.

"Lady Christina was informing me that you have set a wedding date." Trying to appear interested, Richard could not help but notice how Lady Newfield drew Lady Christina away, allowing both himself and Mr. Markham to talk without interruption. "That must be very pleasing for you."

Mr. Markham smiled, his conceit returning almost at once. "I am very pleased with all these arrangements," he said in a matter of fact tone. "Lady Christina is an excellent creature and shall make me a most satisfactory wife, I am sure."

"I am certain she will," Richard replied, ignoring just how tightly his heart was being squeezed. "Might I ask as to where you will live after the marriage takes place?"

Mr. Markham narrowed his eyes as though Richard had asked a most inappropriate question. A little surprised, Richard said nothing more, keeping his expression open and his frame relaxed.

"I am not certain as yet," Mr. Markham replied after a moment. "We may travel for a time."

This sent a spiral of alarm whirling through Richard, but he did not allow it to make its way into his expression. "I see," he said with a small smile. "There are a good many delights away from England's shores, and I am sure Lady Christina would be delighted to see some of them."

Snorting, Mr. Markham waved a hand. "You surely cannot think that I would do such a thing for *her* benefit?" he asked as though Richard was being more than foolish. "Indeed, it is not! She is my wife, so of course, she will attend with me, but anywhere we are to go will be entirely for my own sake." He shrugged. "Business matters and the like, you understand. It does not matter to me one jot as to where my wife might wish to go."

Richard clenched his jaw tight, biting back his hard response. There was clearly no love or even a general consideration for Lady Christina, and that made him more than a little angry.

"Once my father passes on, I shall, of course, inherit the Fulham estate," Mr. Markham continued as though this were all he considered when it came to the apparent death of his father. "Then, we shall return to England so that I might claim my title and make all the improvements upon the house that I have long wished for."

Richard lifted one eyebrow as Mr. Markham puffed out his chest for what was the second time that afternoon, wondering if the gentleman was aware that he had given away a good deal more than he had perhaps intended. "You intend to make improvements?" Richard remarked, genuine in his interest. "That is a wise idea, I must say."

Mr. Markham's expression darkened for a moment. "I have long had intentions to do so, yes," he muttered, looking away from Richard. "But I have not had the opportunity as yet."

Richard's interest held steady as he tried to think of what he might be able to say that would encourage Mr. Markham to speak all the more openly.

"My father has never been one to consider the future," Mr. Markham continued, his gaze now firmly fixed on his father, who was laughing loudly at something. "I must do so, however. So that the title may hold."

"Is that not something we all must do?" Richard queried with a small half-smile. "We must aim to achieve greater things than those who have gone before us, even our very own fathers!"

Mr. Markham lifted an eyebrow and looked at Richard with evident consideration. "Indeed," he said slowly as though deliberating whether or not Richard himself might someone with whom he could discuss such ideas with. "That is my thought precisely." With a sigh, he turned a little, stepping closer to Richard and speaking a good deal more quietly, his eyes a trifle slanted.

"Might I ask, Lord Harlow, whether or not you faced any particular challenges when you inherited the title?" Mr. Markham asked, his eyes darting away from Richard for a moment as though he feared his father would overhear him. "I confess that I do not have a great deal of experience with such matters and very few people to whom I might speak." He looked at Richard with questions in his eyes, to the point that Richard wanted to laugh aloud at the strange camaraderie that Mr. Markham obviously felt was now growing between them.

"I did, certainly," he said with as much gravity as he could. Recalling what Lady Christina had told him about what she had overheard Lord Sturrock say, Richard took a chance and, leaning a little closer, made certain that a most severe expression wrote itself across his face. "In fact," he said heavily, "my father had some severe debts, which I was forced to repay." Shaking his head and praying that would not bring down some sort of curse upon his head for lying in such a fashion, Richard let out a long sigh. "I confess that I was mortified, having been entirely unaware of such debts. Having come into the title, I then shortly received letters demanding payment. Can you imagine it?"

Mr. Markham's dark eyes were fixed to Richard's, his jaw set and a slight frown flickering across his brow. Richard did not know whether or not he had said the right thing but continued regardless, praying that Mr. Markham would take this as an opportunity to speak a little more openly than before.

"I do not mind confessing that I found it a very difficult situation indeed," Richard finished. "Not only was I trying to establish myself as the new viscount, but I was also mourning the loss of my father. To then be given another heavy burden was almost more than I could bear."

"That is something that I will admit to being somewhat concerned about," Mr. Markham muttered, rubbing one finger over his chin as he studied Richard carefully. He took a breath, giving Richard the impression that he was considering whether or not to say more. Inwardly, Richard prayed that he would do so, hopeful that his efforts would not be in vain.

Eventually, Mr. Markham seemed to make up his mind. He cleared his throat, set his shoulders, and put his hands behind his back.

"Perhaps, Lord Harlow, you might be willing to discuss this matter with me further," he said, sending a spiral of hope up into Richard's heart. "Only if you are willing, of course."

Richard shrugged, not wanting to seem too eager. "If I can be of some assistance, then certainly," he said as Mr. Markham nodded—although he did not smile.

"Perhaps we might meet at Whites one evening—let us say after Lord Winchester's ball?" Mr. Markham suggested as Richard nodded. "Thank you, Lord Harlow. You have been very helpful, indeed."

Murmuring something about how he had done nothing much thus far, Richard bade Mr. Markham a good evening and meandered back through the room, struggling to keep the smile from his face. Had it not been for Lady Christina, he would never have known to mention the debts and, had he not done that, he would never have had Mr. Markham speak in such a way. Richard had no knowledge of what Mr. Markham might want to speak to him about, but, regardless, he was thrilled with the progress they had made. If he was lucky, then this meeting with Mr. Markham in two days might be the beginning of something truly significant.

"Good evening, Lady Christina."

The two days that he had been separated from Lady Christina had been two days of torment. He had not had any opportunity to meet with her, for Lady Christina had been caught up with various engagements with her betrothed. It seemed to Richard as though Mr. Markham wanted to make certain that Lady Christina was nowhere but by his side. The joy and relief mingling within him upon seeing her was so wonderful, he could not help but capture her hand, bow over it, and allow his lips to touch her skin. The urge to pull her into his arms and to hold her close filled him, but with an effort, he let go of her hand and stepped back.

"Good evening, Lord Harlow," came the quiet reply, even though her eyes were shining as she looked up at him. "It has felt like an age since I have last set eyes upon you."

Richard nodded, feeling much of the same sentiment. "I did not even have the opportunity to tell you of what occurred, Lady Christina," he said, glad that the business of the ball had allowed them both an opportunity to speak together. "Mr. Markham is to meet me this evening so that we might discuss something related to his father's debts—or some circumstance that is troubling him."

Lady Christina's eyes flared wide with astonishment. "Truly?"

"Truly," he said, wishing he could embrace her. "There is hope, it seems, Lady Christina. Lord Prestwick's plans have proven to be wise ones indeed."

"I am so very relieved," Lady Christina breathed, her fingers finding his and twining through them, the darkness of the shadows to their left hiding the gesture. "What do you think he will say?"

"I cannot imagine," Richard replied, seeing how Lady Newfield stood nearby but did not look over towards them. "But I shall write to you just as soon as I know."

Lady Christina said nothing, her face tilted towards his, looking up at him and smiling gently. There was such warmth and tenderness in his eyes that he could barely move, feeling his heart ache with all that he felt for her. He didn't want to move away, did not want to remove himself from her, and yet knew that he would soon have to do so.

"Lady Christina," he said, softly, "I..." The words he wanted to speak died on his lips, finding his heart too full of emotion to express it properly. Instead, she nodded, perhaps aware of what it was he had intended to say, her hand still holding his.

"Perhaps you might wish to sign my dance card?" she asked, making him smile as she reluctantly let his hand free and held it out towards him. "I have not, as yet, had any name written down upon them." Her lips twisted, and she frowned. "Save for Mr. Markham, of course."

Seeing that Mr. Markham had taken the first waltz, Richard lost no time in writing his name down for the second. The other he chose was the country dance, glad that he would be in Lady Christina's company on at least two more occasions this evening. "I have chosen two," he said, handing it back to her, lifting his head and letting out a long breath as he looked around at everyone. "In fact, I—"

Stopping dead, he let his eyes follow Mr. Markham, noting with interest that he was walking alongside a young lady who was, it seemed, entirely unchaperoned.

"What is it?" Lady Christina asked, her hand now on his arm, her fingers tight on his. "Have you seen something that is of concern?"

Richard did not immediately answer but waited until he had seen where Mr. Markham went before letting his gaze turn back to Lady Christina.

"I have just seen your betrothed leave the ball with a young lady by his side," he said, seeing how her brows shot upwards. "It may be a little daring, Lady Christina, but might I suggest that we go after them at once?"

"And see who she is?" Lady Christina asked, color rushing into her cheeks.

Offering her his arm, Richard let his lips curve to one side. "More than that, Lady Christina," he said quietly. "Precisely what it is they are doing."

CHAPTER TEN

Christina did not know what to think, her arm in Lord Harlow's as she walked alongside him, with Lady Newfield following quickly behind. Lord Harlow had murmured to Lady Newfield what he had seen and there had not been a moment's hesitation from Lady Newfield herself. Instead, she had been eager to hurry Christina along, an expectation in her eyes that Christina herself was beginning to feel.

Her mind whirled as Lord Harlow led them through the ballroom, leading her up a short staircase and through a door. Christina did not know where it led, but she went willingly, her heart pounding with anticipation as the door swung open before her.

Disappointment rose at once as she saw nothing but a few doors and a couple of footmen standing in front of them. Of Mr. Markham and this young lady, she could see no sign.

"They must have gone somewhere," Lord Harlow

murmured, reaching across to pat her hand. "Wait a moment, Lady Christina, if you please."

Christina nodded and waited silently as Lord Harlow spoke quickly to a footman. Nervous anxiety rose within her, and she waited, her fingers twisting in front of her. She was not, of course, in any way upset or offended that Mr. Markham had gone off with another lady, although she had to confess a little concern over the lady herself. If she was unchaperoned, as Lord Harlow had said, then there was surely a worry as to *why* she was without a companion. The last thing Christina wanted to know about her betrothed was that he was the sort of gentleman inclined towards seeking a mistress or taking his pleasure with whomever he wished, regardless of the lady in question's safety or reputation.

"This way."

Lord Harlow held out a hand to her, and Christina took it at once, her steps quickening as he hurried her along the hallway. No one spoke for some moments, Lord Harlow's hand holding hers with a strength and yet a gentleness that spoke of his affection for her. Hope and anticipation began to wind through her as her steps slowed, Lord Harlow pointing out one door in particular.

"This is where Mr. Markham went," Lord Harlow murmured as Christina's heart began to pound furiously. "The footman was quite certain of it."

Christina hesitated, pulling Lord Harlow back as he made to push the already ajar door open a little further.

"Wait," she said, quietly, one hand to her lips as he looked down at her. Gesturing that they ought only to listen rather than storm into the room and demand to know what Mr. Markham was doing, she carefully let go of Lord Harlow's hand and moved a little closer to the door.

Making sure to stay out of sight, she held her breath and tried to listen carefully, but all she could hear was the pounding of her heart. Breathing very slowly and carefully, she waited until her heart was no longer as loud nor as furious, closing her eyes to keep herself steady.

When she opened her eyes, Lord Harlow stood opposite her, leaning against the wall, with Lady Newfield just behind him. Forcing herself to pay attention to what she might hear rather than on Lord Harlow, Christina waited and focused entirely on what snatches of conversation floated towards them.

"There is nothing I can do, but surely you know just how much I do not desire this."

Her eyes widened. Mr. Markham was speaking with a good deal more emotion in his voice than she had ever heard before. There was no arrogance in his tone, no smudge of conceit. Instead, there was a note of desperation there, and, as she continued to listen, Christina was certain she could hear a hint of sadness.

"I have no other choice," Mr. Markham said as though he were begging someone to believe him. "If I could change the situation, then I would do so, but you must know that I—"

"Perhaps if my husband had not left me a poor widow, then your father might..." Christina could not hear the rest of the sentence, her brows lowering as she frowned, trying to understand what was being said. Why was Mr. Markham so markedly different in speaking to this particular lady? What was it that he was so eager to change? The desire to push her way into the room and to discover who was speaking to him was strong, but Christina knew she could not. Instead, she began to step away, and, after a moment, Lord Harlow followed, with Lady Newfield coming after.

Christina said nothing, keeping her voice silenced until they had made their way back into the ballroom. As they had walked into the ballroom, once the noise of the guests and the laughter and the music washed over them, she found herself letting out a breath she had not realized she was holding.

Turning to Lord Harlow, she saw the astonishment still written on his face, looking from one side of the room to the next as though he were trying to work out what to say about what they had heard. Christina's mind was whirring, and, from the expression on Lady Newfield's face, she too was just as surprised as Christina.

"My goodness," Lady Newfield murmured, speaking for the first time since they had returned to the ballroom. "Whatever was that odd meeting?"

Lord Harlow shook his head and shrugged. "I do not know," he said slowly. "We should move away, however, so that when they return, we may take note of the lady."

Christina nodded hurriedly and moved away from the stairs and back into the shadows where they had stood previously. Seeing the way Lord Harlow was shaking his head to himself, Christina could not help but smile.

"You are as surprised as I, I think," she said, as Lord

Harlow dragged his eyes back to her for a moment, a rueful grin on his face. "I have never heard Mr. Markham speak in such a fashion before!"

"If I had not known that it was Mr. Markham within, I should not have believed it," Lord Harlow answered with a smile. "And I must confess, I wonder what it is that the lady was speaking of."

"At least we know now why she was unaccompanied," Lady Newfield remarked, glancing over her shoulder towards the stairs. "A widow, did she not say?"

Christina nodded. "And not a wealthy one, although why that should matter, I cannot say."

Lord Harlow caught his breath, his hand reaching out to grasp her hand. "Unless," he gasped, his eyes wide, "there is an attachment there that he cannot speak of to anyone." His fingers gentled on hers. "Much like there is between us, Lady Christina."

Christina stared back at him, wondering if Lord Harlow was truly aware of what he was suggesting. She could not imagine Mr. Markham to have such an affection for a lady.

"It might sound particularly foolish, given what we know of him, but we must consider the possibility," Lord Harlow continued, only for Lady Newfield to grasp Christina's arm, her head turned towards the stairs.

Instantly, Lord Harlow turned, letting go of Christina's hand. Christina watched carefully, seeing Mr. Markham stepping down into the ballroom, that supercilious smile back on his face. She could barely believe that what she had heard from within that room had come from Mr. Markham's lips, not when she saw him as he was now.

"Do you think the lady will have left?" Lady Newfield asked as Lord Harlow shook his head.

"She will return, but, most likely, a few minutes later than he," he said quietly, as Christina watched Mr. Markham walk a little further into the room—although, much to her relief, he stepped away from them rather than towards them. "Her reputation will not be of particular interest to others, given she is already a widow—and, from what it seems, a somewhat impoverished one." He made to say more, only for the door to open again, and a young lady begin to descend the steps.

Christina studied her closely, not recognizing the lady at all. She had fair hair, her cheeks were rosy, but, from what Christina could see, there was a hint of sorrow about her expression. Christina glanced at Lady Newfield, feeling the tightness of her great-aunt's grasp on her arm.

"Do you know the lady?" she asked as Lord Harlow frowned, shaking his head in answer to her question.

"I am not acquainted with her, no," he said as Lady Newfield turned back to them, her expression more than a little excited.

"I most *certainly* am!" Lady Newfield said as Christina's heart quickened with excitement. "That is Lady Burroughs. She is the late wife of Viscount Burroughs, who was rather old when he wed her." She shook her head, a frown beginning to form over her brow. "There was a lot of disapproval, given Lord Burroughs had already wed two other ladies—both of whom passed away shortly after their marriage. He was much too old for her, but Lady Burroughs' father was quite willing to remove the encumbrance of a daughter as yet unwed from himself and so agreed to the marriage."

Christina let out a slow breath, wondering what it was that Mr. Markham could have discussed with the lady. "I see."

"Although what she was doing speaking to Mr. Markham, I cannot imagine," Lady Newfield answered, looking towards Lord Harlow with interest. "Unless it is what Lord Harlow has suggested."

Christina shook her head. "Surely, it cannot be that," she said with a shake of her head. "I cannot believe that there is any sort of attachment between them!"

"And yet, that might well be the only explanation," Lord Harlow remarked slowly, turning back to face her. "He spoke of being unable to change the situation but being very eager to do so. There was regret in his voice."

"And Lady Burroughs implied that perhaps Lord Fulham might be more contented with her should she have wealth," Lady Newfield said, her eyes brightening as she smiled at Christina. "I think, despite our astonishment at this situation, it may be as has been suggested."

Christina closed her eyes, shaking her head at the idea. "But even if it is so," she answered, "there is nothing that can be done. Lord Fulham will not agree to his son's marriage to anyone who has no wealth. And even if we were to confront him about what we have overheard, the debt my father owes still remains." Her heart began to sink, despair beginning to grow within her. "It is to Lord Fulham that he owes the debt, not to Mr. Markham."

Lord Harlow smiled warmly despite the heaviness of her words.

"Do not give up so quickly, Lady Christina," he told her. "We have an opportunity to, perhaps, speak openly to Mr. Markham. To have him tell us the truth of his situation. I must begin to believe that the façade he presents is nothing more than a mask; a mask that he places upon himself in order to ensure that he behaves as is expected."

Christina frowned. "A gentleman is obedient to no one but himself," she said, speaking from what she knew. "What expectations can you speak of?" She knew very well that most gentlemen behaved appropriately at public functions but that, during their times away from the public eye, they often did as they wished. A lady could be ruined by a simple mistake, whereas a gentleman could do as he pleased and never really be thrown from society as a lady might.

Lord Harlow's smile remained, and, daringly, he reached out to brush his fingers down her cheek. "A gentleman can be forced to abide by the wishes of his father," he said with an air of understanding that told her he had been subject to such a situation. "And Lord Fulham does not appear to be a man able to set aside his own wishes, but rather seems to focus entirely on what he wants—and, therefore, he has high expectations for his son."

"I can hardly believe that to be true," Christina answered, her skin warm and her heart beating furiously at the merest touch of his hand. "But if it is as you say, how are we to have him admit to it?"

Lord Harlow hesitated. "I am not yet sure," he told her honestly. "But I shall, however, endeavor to discover a little more about him this evening." His smile was bright, and the light in his eyes brought a fresh hope to her heart. "And mayhap, you might acquaint yourself with Lady Burroughs?"

"An excellent idea, Lord Harlow!" Lady Newfield declared as Christina began to smile. "That may, in fact, unsettle Mr. Markham all the more—to the point that he might be more willing to speak openly to you later this evening."

Lord Harlow beamed but then shook his head, his smile fading away. "I do not like having to bid you farewell, Lady Christina, but I must hope that, very soon, there shall be no barriers between us."

"I cannot wait for that day," she told him truthfully. "And I must now begin to believe that it is not so far away."

"It is not," he swore, taking her hand and bowing over it again, her heart beginning to ache as she realized their time together was now at an end—at least, for the moment. "I shall write to you tomorrow, Lady Christina."

"I shall be waiting," she told him, regret within her heart as she watched him walk away.

Lady Newfield stepped towards her at once, clearly aware that there was a sorrow within Christina's heart at that moment.

"Shall we go to speak to Lady Burroughs?" she asked, catching Christina's attention and pulling her away from the shadows. "You shall dance with Lord Harlow very soon, and that, I am sure, must please you."

It was something Christina had quite forgotten and, thus encouraged, she slipped her arm through Lady Newfield's, and they began to make their way through the ballroom.

"I am acquainted with Lady Burroughs through my friendship with her mother, Lady Sullinger," Lady Newfield explained, her steps slow but her attention fixed on finding the lady in question. "Lady Sullinger often told me of her sorrow over her daughter's betrothal and her subsequent marriage." Her brows drew together, and her mouth tightened. "Gentlemen such as Lord Sullinger are entirely selfish, ignorant, and conceited. He should never have forced his daughter into such a marriage, but he only looked to his own wellbeing rather than that of his daughter."

"He is not the first gentleman to have done so, and certainly will not be the last," Christina murmured. "My own father has always been very good to me, I admit. I have been lucky."

Lady Newfield turned her head to look at her, her lip caught between her teeth for a moment, but before she could say anything, her eyes widened, and she stopped dead.

"I see her," she said, halting Christina and herself. "Come, this way." She patted Christina's arm. "Allow me to make the introductions."

"Of course," Christina murmured, a tight ball settling in her stomach as they made their way together across the room. Lady Newfield meandered slowly, having no obvious intention, but Christina could feel the tension in her great-aunt's arm.

"Ah, Lady Burroughs, is it not?"

Lady Newfield stopped and bobbed a quick curtsy as Lady Burroughs turned to them, a look of confusion on her face. It quickly faded away as Lady Newfield introduced herself again, enquiring as to how Lady Burroughs' mother fared. As Lady Burroughs answered, her voice low and soft, Christina took a moment to study the lady. She appeared to be only a few years older than Christina —young indeed for a widow—with her fair hair curled at the back of her head, her eyes gentle, and a grace about her that could almost be felt.

Christina felt no wariness whatsoever.

"You must forgive my rudeness," Lady Newfield said after Lady Burroughs had finished speaking. "Please, allow me to introduce Lady Christina. She is the daughter of the Earl of Enfield and my great-niece."

A pair of blue eyes became fixed to Christina's, and she curtsied quickly, noting that it took Lady Burroughs a few moments to return the gesture. When the lady raised her eyes again, there was no smile on her face. In fact, she did not appear to be at all delighted to meet Christina.

"It is very good to meet you," Christina said after a moment or two of silence. "I am sorry to hear that your husband has passed away. That must be very difficult for you."

Lady Burroughs flinched as though Christina had injured her. "It was over a year ago," she said, a little tightly. "I do not feel any particular grief."

It was a cold response, and Christina was a little

surprised by it, although she tried to erase any indication of it from her expression.

"All the same, that must be difficult," Lady Newfield said with a kindness in her voice that Lady Burroughs could not help but respond to. A small, sad smile crept over her face, and she nodded, looking back at Lady Newfield rather than focusing on Christina.

"It has been, yes," she said softly. "After my year of mourning, I came back to society and found that all was not as I had expected." As she spoke, her gaze slid towards Christina, but Christina only smiled, not at all eager to make the lady aware that she had an inkling as to what she was referring.

"Society is not as I thought either," Christina answered, wondering if this might make Lady Burroughs a little warmer in her behavior towards her.

"But you are engaged, are you not?" Lady Burroughs asked, a little sharp in her tone. "That is surely what society expects? And what you have expected?"

"Indeed not," Christina replied, shaking her head. "My own dear father was to allow me to make my own choice in matrimony, only for circumstances to change." Knowing that she ought not to speak with such honesty to someone she had only just been introduced to, Christina held back her next words with great difficulty. Instead, she merely glanced towards Lady Newfield, who nodded with evident sympathy.

"You simply *must* allow me to call upon you, Lady Burroughs," Lady Newfield said warmly. "I should like to see your mother again, of course, but if she is still at home, then that would prove a little more difficult, would it not?"

This made Lady Burroughs laugh. "Yes, it would, given the estate is so far away from London." She smiled at Lady Newfield, clearly glad to have been offered the invitation. "I should like you to call, Lady Newfield. Whenever you would wish it." Her eyes slid slowly towards Christina. "And, of course, you must bring your niece."

This was said with a good deal less fervor, but that did not stop Lady Newfield from accepting with great enthusiasm.

"I look forward to becoming a little better acquainted with you, Lady Burroughs," Christina said before Lady Burroughs then excused herself. As she stepped away, Christina caught sight of her betrothed.

"It seems Mr. Markham is watching us, Lady Newfield," she said softly, turning her whole body away from him whilst Lady Newfield's eyes sought him out amongst the crowd. "Is he there still?"

Lady Newfield nodded but smiled as though they were talking of something quite lovely. "His eyes fixed upon Lady Burroughs as she walked away and then returned to you," she told Christina, who felt an uncomfortable prickling running up her spine. "Now he has turned away from you also. He is walking in the opposite direction, in fact."

"That is odd, indeed," Christina murmured, looking down at her dance card. "For we were to dance the very next dance—the first waltz of the evening."

Lady Newfield chuckled, and Christina felt her heart

lift within her chest. Whatever they had stumbled upon, it might well be the answer to her struggle against her unwelcome marriage.

"He appeared deeply unsettled, I will say," Lady Newfield finished, sounding more than a little satisfied. "Let us hope that Lord Harlow finds out all that he can from Mr. Markham. Mark my words, Christina. We have stumbled upon something very interesting indeed!"

CHAPTER ELEVEN

To have not only spoken at length to Lady Christina, but to have danced with her twice, had left Richard with a feeling of joy in his heart. The evening had gone a good deal better than he had expected, for whatever Mr. Markham had been speaking of to Lady Burroughs, it was clearly of great importance. Finally, he felt as though he could hold onto something tangible, something that would give him a great hope for resolving this situation. All he had to do now was listen to Mr. Markham and allow him to speak as freely as he wished.

Whites was quite busy by the time Richard entered it, with many of the gentlemen already well into their cups. Determined to keep his mind clear, Richard ordered only one small brandy before requesting to know whether or not one Mr. Markham had already entered. Being told that the gentleman had not done so, he found himself a seat in a quiet corner, rested his head back, and let out a long breath.

"Lord Sturrock," he heard someone say. "Another whisky?"

Instantly, Richard's head lifted and he looked all around him, wondering where Lord Sturrock might be. Being quite certain that he had been introduced to him only the once, it took a moment or two for Richard to recognize him. The man was sitting forward in his chair, one elbow on his knee with his other hand gesticulating wildly as he held an empty brandy glass tightly within it. Laughing furiously, he threw his head back and slapped his knee, making Richard smile broadly. If he was to speak to Lord Sturrock—for he had not done so as yet— then now was a perfect opportunity to do so. And if Mr. Markham saw them in conversation, then all the better!

"Lord Sturrock!" he exclaimed, pushing himself out of his chair and coming across the room to the gentleman. "Were you at the ball this evening?"

Lord Sturrock's eyes took a moment to focus on him before a smile slid across his face.

"Lord Harlow!" he cried, not rising from his chair. "No, I was not at the ball. I was with Lord Seaton for dinner this evening, as well as a few other guests." He grinned, his words a little slurred. "It was, I will admit, an excellent evening."

"I am glad to hear it," Richard replied, sitting down near to Lord Sturrock as the gentlemen Lord Sturrock had been speaking with began to talk amongst themselves. "I had an enjoyable evening also, although perhaps not as good as your own!"

Lord Sturrock grinned and sat back in his chair. "There are to be a few card games, I am sure," he said, gesturing to the busy room. "Or the finest French brandy whenever you wish!"

Richard chuckled but waved a hand no. "I cannot," he said with a small sigh. "I am to meet with Mr. Markham. Not for anything in particular, you understand, but I cannot simply join a game of cards."

Immediately, the smile faded from Lord Sturrock's face. "Mr. Markham is to join you here?" he asked, a little darkly. "This evening?"

"Yes, very shortly, I hope," Richard replied easily. "Are you acquainted with him?" He kept his tone light, hoping that this would prompt Lord Sturrock, and, after a few moments, it seemed he was successful.

"I am acquainted, yes," Lord Sturrock said heavily. "An unfortunate acquaintance, however."

Richard lifted one eyebrow. "Oh?"

Lord Sturrock shook his head and ran one hand through his hair, sending it in a messy heap. "That particular gentleman has promised me that he will repay a hefty debt, and, as yet, he has not managed to do so," he said, the smile completely faded now. "The promises are nothing more than empty air."

Shrugging, Richard spread his hands. "Then demand it," he said as though it were as simple as that. "Force it from him in some way."

At this remark, Lord Sturrock threw his head back and sighed heavily as though every last part of his breath was being pulled from him.

"I will not do that," he said, his speech still a little slurred.

"And why not?"

Again came that heavy breath, and Richard found himself holding his, wondering what it was that Lord Sturrock was about to reveal.

"Because I am trying to be gentlemanly about things," he said, deflating Richard's hopes somewhat. "I do not like to demand, even when it is money that I am owed."

"That is very good of you," Richard remarked, sitting back in his seat. "I do not think that I would be as eager to do so."

A small shrug met his words. "It is not Mr. Markham's fault, in many ways," Lord Sturrock said, closing his eyes. "Therefore, I must not behave improperly."

Richard made to say more, a small movement catching his eye. As he turned his head, he saw Mr. Markham stop dead, looking at them both with wide eyes.

"Ah, there is Mr. Markham now," Richard said in a very jovial manner. "Do excuse me, Lord Sturrock—and I wish you luck in whatever card games you intend to play this evening!"

Lord Sturrock chuckled but kept his eyes closed. "I thank you, Lord Harlow. Good evening."

"Good evening," Richard murmured, rising to his feet and making his way towards Mr. Markham. As he drew nearer, he saw how Mr. Markham dropped his gaze for a moment, hearing him clear his throat. Evidently, the man was doing all he could to regain his composure.

"Good evening, Mr. Markham!" Richard exclaimed, trying to sound as amiable as possible. "Do you have a drink to hand? They have some of the best brandy here, I must confess." He smiled jovially, but the smile that was returned was nothing more than a flicker.

"Good evening," Mr. Markham said, his eyes drifting across to where Richard had been sitting. "You have been speaking to Lord Sturrock, I see?"

Richard shrugged. "I am not particularly well acquainted with him, but I thought it best to greet him," he replied. "Now, shall we sit down somewhere? I am rather fatigued after the ball this evening, as I am sure you must be also!"

Mr. Markham said nothing but instead walked past Richard towards the corner of the room, where it was quieter. He sat down hard, his face set and his hands curling tightly around the arms of the chair.

Richard chose to keep a jovial tone.

"Lord Sturrock was just informing me that there are to be a few games of cards this evening," he said, gesturing back towards the fellow. "If you are interested, of course."

"I am not interested in going anywhere near Lord Sturrock," Mr. Markham bit back before closing his eyes and turning his head away, evidently aware that he had said more than he ought. Inwardly, Richard grinned, knowing full well that he had an opportunity now to question what had been said.

"Is that so?" he murmured, tilting his head just a little. "Has the man injured you in some way?" When Mr. Markham did not immediately answer, Richard lifted one shoulder in a small shrug. "There is obviously some upset between you, although I do not mean to pry."

It took a few minutes for Mr. Markham to speak again. His eyes were darting from one place to the next, his brows low and his jaw working furiously.

"You will think it foolish, Lord Harlow, for it sounds as though it is my own doing that has placed difficulty between us, but it is not entirely as it first appears."

Spreading his hands, Richard spoke honestly. "I shall not judge whatever it is you wish to express," he told the man. "I am well aware that, in many situations, there is more than one perspective."

Mr. Markham's eyes shot to Richard's. "That is it precisely," he acknowledged slowly. "It appears as though I owe a great debt to Lord Sturrock, and, whilst that is in some ways true, it is not exactly as it sounds."

Wondering if this was the reason that Lord Fulham had demanded that his son marry a lady above his station, with what would be a very large dowry also, Richard nodded in what he hoped would appear to be a most understanding manner. "I see," he said, choosing his words with great care. "Then you are frustrated with Lord Sturrock for continually expressing his eagerness for you to pay this debt, when you know all too well that it is not one of your own doing."

A muscle twitched in Mr. Markham's cheek. "No, that is not quite as it is," he answered gravely. "The debt *is* my own, but it was not given to me of my own choosing." Seeming to relax just a little, he let out a pained sigh and sat forward in his chair, one hand running through his hair. "My father, Lord Fulham, has more than one large debt that he has acquired," he said as Richard fought the urge to ask as many questions as he could. "However, when the time comes for him to write a vowel or to sign a document stating he will pay what he owes, he does not place the debt on *his* shoulders, but rather on mine."

Much to Richard's surprise, he felt a faint stirring of sympathy within his chest as he considered this. It was clearly a very heavy burden on Mr. Markham's shoulders, and one, certainly, that he ought not to bear.

"I do not quite understand," Richard replied, frowning. "Why does your father do this? And do the gentlemen to whom he owes these debts agree to his lack of responsibility?"

Mr. Markham shrugged. "They care not. I believe, in fact, that some of them are relieved, given my father is not the sort of gentleman who willingly takes such responsibility and acts without thought or consideration."

"Whereas you do what you can to manage such debts with responsibility," Richard finished, his brows still low. "But how can you do so if you are not yet Baron Fulham?"

Another sigh emanated from Mr. Markham. "I do what I can with what I have," he said. "I have very little left of my own coffers, whilst my father remains in sole control of the estate and all that goes with it. He does not care about whether or not I am solvent, for it simply means that he has more money with which to spend."

Richard's frown deepened. "But that is hardly fair!" he exclaimed as Mr. Markham nodded and gave him a wry smile.

"It is not fair at all," he answered heavily, spreading his hands. "But what am I to do? I have paid off a good many debts, and yet my father accumulates more. Lord Sturrock has the greatest amount still owed, and he is continually demanding that I repay him, but I have nothing left to give him."

This was a very strange situation, indeed, Richard considered, gesturing to a footman to bring them both a glass of brandy. He had been quite determined to hate Mr. Markham for what he had done, for how he had stepped in the way of Richard's own intentions with Lady Christina. And now, however, he found himself feeling a little sorry for the man as the story he had told had pulled compassion from Richard's heart.

"My father is inclined towards greatness," Mr. Markham muttered, accepting the glass of brandy from the footman. "He wants to be the sort of gentleman who can live as he pleases, who had thrown around his coffers with na'ar a thought. My mother is delighted with this circumstance and only encourages him to continue, despite my urgings to the contrary."

"Which is why Lord Fulham arranged for your betrothal to Lady Christina," Richard murmured, slowly beginning to see the situation as it really was. "He wants the family line to have excellent connections within it and, alongside that, the wealth that such connections will bring."

Mr. Markham let out a small, scornful laugh. "It appears you have the measure of my father already, Lord Harlow," he said, passing a hand over his eyes. "I, of course, am expected to behave in a certain manner, expected to do as I am asked without question." Another heavy sigh ripped from his lips. "And I do so for fear of what might occur if I do not."

"I understand," Richard replied with a small smile. "My father was similar in a good many ways, I think!" This was not entirely true, for Richard's father, whilst stern, had not been as demanding as Richard now made out.

"I have felt as though you understand, Lord Harlow," Mr. Markham remarked, beginning to look a little more relaxed. "I do not have any particularly close acquaintances with whom I could share this matter." His lips tipped in a wry smile. "They all think that I have nothing to complain of, given I am to wed Lady Christina."

The mention of his beloved's name made Richard's stomach tighten with a sudden anger that he struggled to mask. Bringing his brandy to his lips, he drank deeply until the emotion swept from him and he was able to be at his leisure once more.

"I did not mean to bring you here so that I might complain about my father," Mr. Markham remarked a little ruefully. "I did come to ask you about how you dealt with such debts being placed upon you when you took the title." His eyes searched Richard's face, clearly eager —if not desperate—for answers.

Richard allowed himself a heavy sigh. "It was not as difficult as your situation, certainly, but it was trying," he admitted, knowing that here, at least, he spoke the truth. He had not been delighted to discover that he had debts to deal with, not when he had been adjusting to all that life had thrown at him—but he had not had *significant* debts, such as Mr. Markham had described.

Running another hand through his hair, Mr. Markham sighed heavily. "Might I ask how you managed the requests for payment?" he asked, looking at Richard. "I am certain that, when it comes time for me to take the title, I will have so many requests that I will not know where to begin!" His expression became sorrowful. "In fact, I am beginning to fear that there will not be enough funds to cover the debts."

"I see," Richard answered, recalling how Mr. Markham had spoken of taking himself and Lady Christina abroad once they were wed. Was that because he did not wish his father to place any further burdens upon him once he was already married?

"I fear that, once I am wed, my father will continue as he is already," Mr. Markham said as though he had known precisely what Richard had been thinking. "I cannot have the burden of a new wife as well as the heavy weight of his debts."

"And thus you intend to travel with your wife until your father has passed," Richard murmured as Mr. Markham nodded. "Precisely so that he cannot do as you suspect."

Nodding, Mr. Markham squeezed his eyes closed, his jaw working furiously. Richard remained silent, wondering what struggles were going on within the fellow and realizing that he had no true understanding of Mr. Markham at all. He had thought him arrogant, selfish, and entirely willing to go along with what had been planned by his father. In fact, Richard had believed that Mr. Markham had not only agreed to but perhaps had planned this situation with Lady Christina, only to realize now that the gentleman had not had any choice in the matter. Was he just as shocked as Lady Christina? Was he just as unwilling?

"Whatever advice you can give me regarding such matters with the debts, finances, and other matters when taking the title, I would be very grateful indeed," Mr. Markham said, slowly opening his eyes and looking at Richard. "It often weighs heavily on my mind, even though that time might be some distance away."

Nodding, Richard decided that the only thing he could do would be to speak openly to Mr. Markham and to give him as much advice as he could. It was obvious that the man had a great weight on his shoulders, and, despite himself, despite the irritation that he felt regarding Lady Christina, Richard also felt eager to impart whatever he could to help Mr. Markham. The situation was a dire one, and he certainly did not envy Mr. Markham in any way.

"Certainly," he said, taking a sip of his brandy. "Let me tell you everything that happened with me."

CHAPTER TWELVE

"I hear you are engaged, Lady Christina."

Christina nodded quickly, smiling warmly at Lady Burroughs but wondering just how much pain it had brought her to speak of such a thing. "I am, yes," she said as Lady Newfield took a sip of her tea and looked at Christina out of the corner of her eye. Christina did not say anything more, recalling that this visit was so that both herself and Lady Newfield might discover all they could about Lady Burroughs' connection to Mr. Markham. Their time with the lady was almost at an end and, as yet, they had not managed to bring him into their conversation. Thankfully, it seemed that Lady Burroughs had done so herself.

"And when is the wedding to take place?" Lady Burroughs asked, her face devoid of expression. "It must be soon, I am sure."

Christina dropped her eyes and did not smile in the hope that Lady Burroughs might understand that there was no joy in her marriage. "It is to be in a few short weeks," she said, her voice low. "I cannot give you any particular details, however, for I am entirely in the dark as to what has been planned."

"Oh, that is unusual, is it not?" Lady Burroughs remarked, although there was no real interest in her voice. "Regardless, Lady Christina, I am certain that you will have great joy in your marriage. Mr. Markham is a very amiable gentleman."

"I do not know him," Christina replied swiftly. "This was arranged entirely by our respective fathers, Lady Burroughs. There has been very little time for me to become acquainted with Mr. Markham, and he, therefore, with me." She looked at Lady Burroughs, letting a flicker of interest rush into her eyes. "But it sounds as though *you* are acquainted with Mr. Markham, Lady Burroughs! Tell me what you know of him, if you would."

Lady Burroughs face paled, and her mouth opened, but no words came out.

"It would be *very* beneficial indeed," Lady Newfield remarked, smiling at Christina. "I know that my great-niece has been a little distressed that she has no knowledge of her betrothed, and whatever you can say will be a great help."

"And bring with it such a great relief," Christina added as Lady Burroughs' mouth closed, and she dropped her head for a moment. Christina and Lady Newfield exchanged glances, with Christina seeing the small smile flickering about Lady Newfield's mouth. If this was as they now suspected, Lady Burroughs felt a great deal for Mr. Markham and might just, in the course of speaking of him, reveal something of it to them both.

That would confirm what they now believed, and, with Lord Harlow having spoken to Mr. Markham at length, they could put what they had learned together and come up with a plan.

"I confess that I do not know a great deal," Lady Burroughs said as though she now wanted to renege on what she had already stated. "I know he is amiable, yes, but that is all."

Christina did not intend to accept such an end to that particular conversation and continued to press the lady. "Might I ask how long you have known him?" she asked, leaning forward just a little in her chair. "I, of course, have only been acquainted with Mr. Markham for as long as we have been engaged!"

Lady Burroughs blinked rapidly but did not smile. "I have been acquainted with him for almost three years," she said, astonishing Christina with her answer, for she had been certain it had only been for a few short weeks. "I met Mr. Markham during the Season I became engaged to Lord Burroughs. Last Season, of course, I was not in London due to the death of my husband."

"Of course," Christina murmured, glancing at Lady Newfield. "And during your acquaintance, you found him to be affable?" She looked down at the floor for a moment. "I confess that I am a little afraid of what my marriage will be like."

"Oh, Lady Christina, there is nothing that you need worry about."

The fervor in Lady Burroughs voice sent a small shudder through Christina, but she did not make a single remark.

"I am *certain* that Mr. Markham will be a very suitable husband," Lady Burroughs continued. "You need not fear that he will be a cruel gentleman, for there is no such viciousness within him."

"He is a little arrogant and conceited, is he not?" Lady Newfield asked rather bluntly. "That is certainly the impression that I have had from him."

Lady Burroughs shook her head. "No, indeed not," she said, her voice softening. "That is only for appearances sake, I am sure of it. After all, must not a gentleman behave in a certain manner in order to gain the respect of others?"

Christina frowned, not quite certain that she believed this last remark. Mr. Markham was certainly arrogant, as far as she was concerned, and had never once treated her with consideration. To hear from Lady Burroughs that she felt Mr. Markham to be entirely the opposite of what she herself had experienced was almost unbelievable.

"I must wish you happiness, Lady Christina," Lady Burroughs finished with an attempt at a warm smile. "I am sure that you will have a wonderful marriage."

WALKING into her father's townhouse—and having discussed what Lady Burroughs had said with Lady Newfield—Christina was all the more astonished to hear from the butler that Lord Harlow had been eagerly anticipating their return for what had been at least an hour.

"I have had him wait in the drawing-room, my lady,"

the butler continued quietly. "Shall I send for refreshments to be brought?"

Christina nodded, her heart beginning to quicken as she wondered what it was that Lord Harlow had discovered. Surely, he would not have appeared at her father's townhouse without explanation had it been something minor.

"Go at once!" Lady Newfield exclaimed, giving Christina a gentle push. "I *must* quickly write a short note, and then I shall join you."

Christina did not stop to consider whether or not this was inappropriate, her anticipation and eagerness to see Lord Harlow overwhelming every thought and emotion. Having handed all her sundries to the butler, she hurried towards the drawing-room, one hand pressed against her chest as the door opened and she stepped inside.

"Christina!"

Lord Harlow breathed her name as he turned towards her. He had been striding up and down the room, it seemed, for he had to turn on his heel to see her. In the next moment, she was in his arms, her head on his shoulder and his arms about her waist. All the breath left her body in an instant, tingling pouring through her as she allowed herself to rest in his arms.

"Oh, Christina," he said again, her name on his lips sending yet another flurry of excited anticipation through her. "I can hardly believe what I have to tell you."

His arms loosened, and he looked down at her, and Christina could barely breathe from the look in his eyes. She had never seen him so animated, so evidently filled with excitement. What she did not expect was for him to drop his head and to kiss her, for his lips to find hers and to rest there for a long moment. Everything began to whirl within her, her hands going around his neck as he held her close.

"There is a clear path ahead," he whispered, resting his forehead against hers for a moment. "I have seen it. I know what we have to do. There is nothing now that we need to do than have Mr. Markham meet with us—and then all will become quite clear. I know it."

Christina could not help but laugh with the joy that spiraled up within her. Even though she did not know nor understand everything that he had said, there was, now, a hope that she could see plainly in his eyes.

"I must tell you what Mr. Markham said," Lord Harlow said eagerly, releasing her and taking her hand, pulling her gently towards the couch. "I think, Lady Christina, that we might have misjudged him."

"Misjudged him?" Christina repeated, astonished. "Goodness, Lord Harlow—that is the second time today I have heard something about Mr. Markham that I could barely believe!"

Lord Harlow's brow furrowed. "The second time?"

"Indeed," she told him as the door opened quietly behind them and Lady Newfield stepped inside, quickly followed by a maid with the refreshments.

"Lady Burroughs insisted that he is amiable, jovial, and will make me a wonderful husband," Christina replied with a wry smile. "I could not believe her, of course."

Lord Harlow chuckled. "But I think you must, Lady Christina," he said, referring back to her formal title now that Lady Newfield was in the room. "For I have spoken to Mr. Markham at length and am now quite certain that there is nothing in his nature that is as it appears."

Lady Newfield sat down and arched one eyebrow. "Is that so?"

Lord Harlow nodded, his grin spreading right across his face and his eyes bright with evident elation. "Let me explain what he spoke to me about," he said, and launched into his story. Christina poured the tea as she listened, her heart filling with both confusion and relief as she heard what Lord Harlow had discovered. She could hardly trust his words, unable to marry the two versions of Mr. Markham—the one she knew herself, and the one that Lord Harlow now spoke of.

"Therefore, I am quite certain that he is not the gentleman we believe him to be," Lord Harlow finished. "He does not *want* this marriage, Lady Christina. And the reason he has acted in such a rude and conceited manner is because this is what his father expects."

"The consequences of him refusing to behave as is expected, however?" Lady Newfield queried. "What should happen if he did not do as he asked?"

Lord Harlow hesitated, then lifted one shoulder. "I believe that he is afraid that his father would press more of a burden upon him as a punishment for refusing to do as is expected," he said, making Christina nod slowly, understanding precisely what Lord Harlow meant. "I must confess that I believe there is a heavy weight of fear on Mr. Markham's heart. He is struggling under the weight of the unfair responsibilities that his father has placed upon his shoulders and is anxious to do all he can to ensure his father does not further such responsibilities."

Christina bit her lip, feeling a small tug of sympathy in her heart and yet eager to ignore it. She did not want to feel any such emotion for Mr. Markham, and yet, it remained.

"You are struggling with what you feel, are you not?" Lord Harlow said gently. "I can tell by the expression that is written on your face, my dear." His smile was soft. "I admit to feeling the very same."

"Truly?" Christina asked, a little surprised. "And you now feel a great deal of compassion for him?"

Lord Harlow lifted one shoulder. "I admit that my consideration has grown, yes. The Mr. Markham that you know, Lady Christina, is not the gentleman that he truly is. There is a façade, a mask that he wears. His heart is not truly in such behavior."

Christina let out a slow breath, letting her mind consider all that had been said. Her skin prickled as she looked up to see Lord Harlow's eyes resting on her, a gentle smile on his face. She wanted so desperately to believe him, but there was still something holding her back.

"So, what must we do?" Christina asked as Lady Newfield began to smile, clearly delighted with this news. "You say that we must meet with Mr. Markham and that, then, everything will become clear?"

Lord Harlow nodded. "I am certain of it," he replied, speaking with such confidence that Christina had no other choice but to believe him. "You say that you went to speak to Lady Burroughs this afternoon?"

Lady Newfield laughed, her eyes sparkling as she looked from Christina to Lord Harlow. "You and I are in agreement, I think, Lord Harlow." Lord Harlow looked towards her and began to chuckle, the sound making Christina begin to smile despite not fully understanding what they meant.

"I think you are correct, Lady Newfield," Lord Harlow replied, looking towards Christina. "Lady Christina, after your meeting today with Lady Burroughs, and after what we witnessed between Mr. Markham and Lady Burroughs at the ball, I must tell you that I believe there is a deep and unbreakable affection between them."

Christina took a moment before she replied, things beginning to twine together, to piece themselves one by one until, finally, she was able to understand completely what was being suggested.

"So you mean to suggest that, should we bring Lady Burroughs and Mr. Markham together and perhaps confront them—"

"In a gentle manner," Lady Newfield interjected.

Christina laughed. "Indeed, in a *gentle* manner, great-aunt, then Mr. Markham will have no other choice but to speak the truth?"

"And confess to us," Lord Harlow added, "that he is desperate to marry Lady Burroughs but has not been able to due to his father's demands and his manipulations."

Lady Newfield nodded. "And because she is without great wealth," she said, gesturing to Christina. "Whereas you, my dear, will bring an excellent dowry, as well as increased status for the family name." She smiled softly.

"And, no doubt, Lord Fulham believes that he will be able to force your father into giving him—or Mr. Markham—more coin when he should need it."

"Indeed," Lord Harlow agreed, a little more solemnly. "He has blackmailed and manipulated your father once. There is no reason he would not attempt to do so again—most likely, using *you* as the leverage he requires to get what he wants."

A cold shiver brushed across Christina's skin. "So you blame this on Lord Fulham entirely," she said, as Lord Harlow nodded. "Therefore, even if we persuade Mr. Markham and Lady Burroughs to speak the truth, to confess their connection, then what can be done?"

Something flickered in Lord Harlow's eyes, and the corner of his mouth tipped up into a small smile. "I have another plan thereafter, Lady Christina," he said gently. "But you must trust me. Let us take one step at a time." His smile grew, and the tenderness in his eyes seemed to reach out and grasp her heart, pushing aside her worry and concern. "Do you think you can trust me enough to wait?"

The answer on her lips was immediate. "Of course I can," she said quickly, as Lady Newfield reached forward to pour a little more tea. "Then let us plan what we must do to bring Lady Burroughs and Mr. Markham together. The sooner we can do this, the happier I shall be."

"The happier we *all* shall be," her great-aunt replied, looking happier than Christina had seen her in some time. "Now, Christina, should you care for more tea?"

CHAPTER THIRTEEN

I t was an effort for Christina to remain just as she had been before with Mr. Markham, not when she now believed that he was not as he appeared.

"I do not intend to stay long, Lady Christina," Mr. Markham said, sniffing and looking about him with evident disdain as though being in her company was not at all enjoyable. "It is not as though I am grateful for your eagerness to have my company."

Christina stiffened despite herself, wanting to bite back a remark but forcing herself not to do so. Sitting down, she gestured for him to do the same, glancing towards Lady Newfield, who sat in the corner of the room as the chaperone.

"It is not too much, I hope," she said as gently as she could. "After all, taking tea is something that we ought to do since we are soon to be wed. There should be time for us to converse, time for us to—"

"Might I ask what it is that you wish to speak of?" Mr. Markham asked, a little irritably. "It is better to come directly to such a conversation rather than to engage in dull and unhelpful remarks that mean very little before one finally comes to what one wishes to say."

It was, Christina realized, a roundabout way of stating that he did not want to speak to her at great length. A practical desire to speak of whatever was on her mind so that he could then depart.

Clearing her throat, Christina smiled tightly at him. "I should like to know a little of what our wedding is to be like," she said as Lady Newfield shifted in her chair, perhaps attempting to remind Mr. Markham that she was present. "After all, you have told me very little, except for the day we are to be wed and where it shall take place." She lifted her chin a notch. "I have asked you for permission to invite some of my closer acquaintances, and you have not, as yet, confirmed whether such invitations will be given to me."

Mr. Markham shifted in his chair and opened his mouth to answer, only to be halted by the arrival of the maid with the tray of refreshments. Tutting under his breath at her evident sluggishness, he waited until she had left the room before speaking.

"There is no need for such invitations, Lady Christina," he told her firmly. "The wedding will be a quiet one. Only those who are required will be present."

Christina shook her head. "I am not contented with such a thing."

"And yet, that is how it shall be," he said in a commanding tone. "The most important details have been well accounted for and dealt with. There is nothing for you to do other than ensure you are prepared for our wedding day."

A flare of irritation ran through Christina's frame, but she stopped herself from saying a single word. Instead, she looked at Lady Newfield and noted the small flick of her eyebrow, which then turned into a frown. It was much easier to believe that Mr. Markham was wearing this outward appearance as a façade when she was being told of it, but much more difficult when he was directly in front of her and speaking to her in such an uncivilized and rude manner.

"If that is all that you wanted to speak of," Mr. Markham said, abruptly rising from his chair, "then I think that I shall—"

"Do sit down, Mr. Markham."

Lady Newfield's voice was commanding, filling the room with her authority, and making Mr. Markham startle in surprise.

"You have come to take tea with your betrothed; there is no reason for you to hurry away like a frightened animal," Lady Newfield continued, the words she chose to describe Mr. Markham making a cloud settle over his brow. "You have only been here for a few minutes!"

Christina held her breath, looking from Lady Newfield to Mr. Markham and wondering whether or not such a remark would have the desired effect. All was silent, tension flooding all around them—until, finally, Mr. Markham sat down.

"I thank you," Lady Newfield said, briskly. "Now, Christina. A little more tea?"

Christina accepted quickly, wondering what they

were now to say to continue a conversation that would keep Mr. Markham from leaving the room again. Both she and Lady Newfield were now eagerly awaiting the arrival of Lord Harlow and Lady Burroughs—although which one would attend the house first, Christina could not say.

"It has been a very fine few days, has it not?" Lady Newfield began, a sense of contentment in her voice as though she knew she had achieved a victory with Mr. Markham. "I do hope you will enjoy such fine weather on the day of your marriage. It is never a good sign, I think, when there is rain."

This rambling monologue continued for some minutes, leaving Christina to sit nervously, waiting desperately for the door to open, for someone—either of the expected guests—to be announced by the butler. If Lady Burroughs did not appear, then there would be a good deal of wasted time and effort, which would then only have to be repeated for a second time.

And then, she heard a scratch at the door.

"Yes?" she called, her voice a little higher than usual. "Come in."

The butler stepped in at once. "My lady, Lord Harlow."

Knowing that the butler had been instructed to show any further guests into the room immediately, Christina rose at once, leaving Lady Newfield to join her whilst Mr. Markham frowned hard but remained in his seat.

"Good afternoon, Lord Harlow," she said as he came into the room. Watching him closely, she saw his eyes flash across the room, taking in who was present and who was not.

"Good afternoon, Lady Christina, Lady Newfield." He bowed and then looked at Mr. Markham. "And Mr. Markham, good afternoon."

Mr. Markham did not rise but merely arched one eyebrow in Lord Harlow's direction. "Good afternoon, Lord Harlow. I did not expect you to be calling on Lady Christina this afternoon."

Lord Harlow chuckled and came to sit down, choosing the seat directly between Mr. Markham and the door. "I know it is unexpected for you, Mr. Markham, but I can assure you that I was quite certain you would be here this afternoon."

Mr. Markham's frown grew. "What can you mean?"

Smiling, Lord Harlow shrugged. "I think that, in a few minutes, Mr. Markham, all will become quite clear."

Silence fell for a few moments, and Christina swallowed hard, quite certain that Mr. Markham would rise and remove himself from the room in an instant—only for a scratch at the door to come again.

Everyone rose, save for Mr. Markham. Lady Newfield moved forward quickly, so that she might encourage Lady Burroughs into the room should she be a little unwilling to remain.

"Lady Burroughs, my lady," the butler murmured before quickly standing aside to allow the lady entry.

Christina spoke words of greeting as Lady Burroughs entered the room, glancing at Mr. Markham for a moment. He had gone stock still, his hands gripping the arms of the chair and his eyes fixed to Lady Burroughs.

There was a pale sheen to his cheeks that had not been there before, and his whole body seemed to be rigid with a tension. As Christina smiled at Lady Burroughs, she saw that she also had gone a pale shade and that her eyes were now fixed to Mr. Markham.

"Please, sit down," Lady Newfield said firmly. "Tea?" She glanced down at the tray and then shook her head. "In fact, I shall send for another tray since we are now so many."

Mr. Markham rose abruptly. "There is no need," he said as Lord Harlow got to his feet also. "I shall take my leave." He turned and inclined his head quickly towards Christina, but she shook her head and took a step towards him.

"You will not leave, Mr. Markham," she said with more confidence in her voice than she felt within. "There are matters that must be discussed, and you *must* inform us of what you know."

For a long moment, Mr. Markham said nothing, his eyes narrowing and his jaw tight. And then, he snorted with evident disdain, turned on his heel, and made to march from the room, only to be prevented by Lord Harlow.

"Please, Mr. Markham," Lord Harlow said, putting his hand out directly in front of Mr. Markham. "Wait. There is more here at stake than you know."

Lady Burroughs sat wide-eyed in her chair, looking from Lord Harlow to Christina and back again. "I do not understand what is happening," she said softly. "Is this meant to be some kind of trick?"

Lady Newfield shook her head. "No, my dear Lady

Burroughs. There is no deception here, save for the one that you and Mr. Markham have been playing with us." The words were gentle and yet filled with meaning. Lady Burroughs startled visibly before turning her head sharply towards Mr. Markham, who was, by now, looking directly at Christina.

"What is the meaning of this, Christina?" he demanded, his eyes filled with anger. "How dare you try to manipulate me in this manner?"

Christina drew in a long breath and tightened her fists in order to steel herself. Now was the time for courage, for bravery. She had to speak the truth and tell him so without hesitation.

"I fear that you are the one being manipulated, Mr. Markham," she said, the whole room falling into silence as she spoke. "Is that not so?" Rising to her feet, her skirts swishing gently, she took a few steps closer to her betrothed. "I know you do not want to marry me but are doing so simply because your father is forcing your hand. I am aware of the difficulties he has placed on you—and yes, you may blame Lord Harlow for my knowledge of this, for he has told me all."

Mr. Markham's jaw set, and for a moment, Christina feared he would swing at Lord Harlow, only for Lady Burroughs to let out a strangled sob, pulling everyone's attention towards her.

"And we are aware that, should you be free to make your own choice, Mr. Markham," Lady Newfield continued, her eyes kind, "you would seek to marry Lady Burroughs. Is that not so?"

Silence wrapped around them all as Mr. Markham

stared furiously at Lady Newfield whilst Lady Burroughs lifted her hands to her mouth and pressed her fingers there as though trying to hold back the words that she knew would reveal the truth. Christina looked towards Lord Harlow and saw his gentle smile and the way that his eyes lifted to hers. Even in this most difficult of moments, even when there was a cloud of tension circling around them all, Christina knew that he felt confident of their victory.

"It does not matter," Mr. Markham grated eventually. "The marriage will go ahead."

Again, a sob came from Lady Burroughs, and she dropped her head—but not before Christina had seen a sheen of tears in her eyes. Her heart began to ache for the lady, knowing all too well the feelings of grief and sorrow that came with being kept from the gentleman you wished desperately to marry.

"But why should you do so?" Lord Harlow asked, his tone rather curious. "Should you continue on as your father demands, then you will not only break your own heart, but the hearts of three others present here today."

Mr. Markham frowned, glancing at Lord Harlow. "I do not know what you mean."

Lord Harlow's expression gentled as he looked at Christina, holding out one hand to her. Christina hurried towards him and took it at once, aware of the astonishment on Mr. Markham's face as he saw their joined hands.

"I love Lady Christina with all of my heart," Lord Harlow said, his words capturing her full attention and making her gasp with delight. "I do not want to allow you to wed her, Markham, not when I know that I can make her happier than you ever could."

Christina looked up at Lord Harlow, sighed, and smiled up into his eyes. "And I long to be Lady Harlow," she said honestly. "I cannot abide the idea of wedding you, Mr. Markham—and," she continued, turning her head to look at him, "I think that you dislike the idea of marriage to me also, given you have a great affection for Lady Burroughs."

Mr. Markham shook his head, running one hand across his forehead. The arrogance and conceit seemed to be pushed from him in an instant, crumpling before her eyes. Christina could not take her eyes from him, astonished at the change in his demeanor. Lord Harlow had been quite right to state that Mr. Markham had been wearing a mask, for now, sitting down heavily in a chair with a dulled expression on his face, was the true Mr. Markham.

"I shall not ask how you have come about this knowledge," Mr. Markham said, his voice low and heavy with frustration. "But I shall say that it is of no use. I may have the greatest of affection for Lady Burroughs, but I cannot wed her. My father has not permitted me to do so. When I first mentioned the lady, I was told, without hesitation, that she would not do. There was not enough wealth to make my father contented—and now that I know the extent of the debts he had placed upon my shoulders, I too can understand that there is no wisdom in the match."

"Even though you care deeply for her?" Christina

asked as Mr. Markham lifted his eyes to hers. "Is money all that concerns you?"

Mr. Markham shook his head. "You cannot understand," he said without any trace of spite or malice in his voice. "I would not be able to provide Lady Burroughs with anything other than debts, poverty, and shame. Not by my own hand, Lady Christina, but by the selfishness of my father." His eyes ran towards Lady Burroughs, who, whilst not sobbing brokenly, was shedding silent tears that ran unabated down her cheeks.

"That is why I understand that the match made by my father—albeit through cruel and manipulative means —must go ahead." One shoulder lifted in a half-shrug. "There is no other way for the Fulham title to remain restored."

Christina's heart began to sink, and she looked up at Lord Harlow in desperation. Were they to have Mr. Markham's confession only for things to remain precisely as they were?

"That does not seem to be particularly fair, Mr. Markham," Lady Newfield said quietly, "and I can assure you that it will not bring you happiness either." Opening his mouth, Mr. Markham made to say something, only for Lady Newfield to hold up one hand, silently asking him to allow her to finish. After a moment, Mr. Markham closed his mouth and sat back again, his arms folded across his chest and his eyes a little hooded.

"It will be an unhappy marriage, Mr. Markham," Lady Newfield continued quietly. "You will leave not only yourself and Lady Christina with sorrow seared into their hearts, but also Lady Burroughs and Lord Harlow."

She tilted her head. "Do you consider wealth and coin to be of a greater importance than that of your own heart? Of greater importance than Lady Burroughs' heart?"

Christina held her breath as she saw Mr. Markham's gaze slide, almost unwillingly, towards Lady Burroughs. His eyes closed tightly, his jaw working furiously and his forehead lined with pain as he saw the red eyes and the white face of the lady he cared for. Her own heart swelling with compassion, Christina leaned a little more into Lord Harlow, feeling as though they were coming ever closer to a precipice to which they might fall into and find no way to escape. Was this her last few moments with Lord Harlow? Would they never be able to grasp the happiness that seemed, at this very moment, only a little out of reach?

"I do not know what else to do," Mr. Markham croaked, his voice now breaking with emotion. "I do not want to marry Lady Christina. I want to marry Lady Burroughs, for it is for her that my heart beats." His eyes opened, and he held Lady Burroughs' gaze. "But what can I do? My father continued to pile debts upon me, and when I come to take the title, I am certain that there will be yet more that I have to deal with. To come to that with very little coin of my own and no easy means of making more is not a situation that I can take Lady Burroughs into."

Christina closed her eyes. Mr. Markham, it seemed, was quite determined that their marriage should go ahead. He could not see a way out of his dark situation and, were she honest with herself, neither could she. The only way Mr. Markham could come to the title with any hope of success was if he had an exceptionally large dowry from his wife, which was precisely what Christina would bring with her into the marriage.

"And what," Lord Harlow said gently, "if I could ensure that such debts were taken care of, Mr. Markham? What if I could make quite certain that your father was unable to continue on as he is at present?"

A sudden flare of hope ran through Christina's chest, and she opened her eyes to look up at him, seeing the gleam in his eye and the smile on his face. Had he a plan that would make certain the agreement between Christina and Mr. Markham would come to an end?

Mr. Markham looked up sharply, his brow knotted. "What can you mean?"

"I mean," Lord Harlow answered, "that if you are willing to trust me, I can assure you that, in a very short space of time, I will have all I need to make certain that Lord Fulham is unable to take on any further debts. The burden will be pulled from your shoulders and you will no longer have the fear that, as you come into the title, you will be weighed down by all manner of debt." His smile grew. "What would you say to that?"

"Oh, Markham!"

Lady Burroughs' breathless exclamation told Christina that the lady was just as filled with hope as she. Mr. Markham seemed torn, turning from Lord Harlow to Lady Burroughs and then back again. Christina pressed one hand to her heart, aware of its thundering and the knot of tension in her stomach. All eyes rested on Mr. Markham as he made his decision.

"You know how much I have longed for this, Lady

Burroughs," he whispered, as Christina closed her eyes, dragging in air to calm her nerves. "I would want nothing more, but..."

"I trust Lady Newfield," Lady Burroughs said desperately. "And if she is involved in this situation in any way, then I know that we can have hope, Markham." She rose and came towards Mr. Markham, who stood up at once, catching the hands that Lady Burroughs held out to him. Christina had never seen him so gentle nor heard such tenderness in his voice as he talked to Lady Burroughs.

"But can it be true?" he asked her as Lady Burroughs eyes filled with tears. "There is a good deal at stake, and if we..." Taking in a deep breath, he let his sentence trail off as he saw something in Lady Burroughs eyes that he could not turn away from. With another deep sigh, he turned to Lord Harlow and wrapped one arm around Lady Burroughs' waist.

"I must take the risk," he said, sounding resigned. "If there is even the smallest hope, the tiniest chance that I can find happiness with Lady Burroughs, then I confess I am willing to do whatever I can."

Christina could not help but break down into tears, turning herself a little more towards Lord Harlow, her head on his shoulder as he held her close for a moment. The tears she cried were ones of relief, ones of sheer joy and overwhelming happiness that all she had hoped for, all she had been desperate to believe in, was now being given to her. Sobs shook her frame for a few minutes, but Lord Harlow held her tightly, allowing her to deal with the emotions that washed all through her. By the time Christina lifted her head, by the time she had found her composure again, it was not only she who had been crying, but also Lady Burroughs and, in fact, Lady Newfield! Mr. Markham looked troubled, clearly uncertain what to do to comfort the lady, whilst Lord Harlow was smiling gently.

"What must we do?" Lady Burroughs asked, pulling a handkerchief from her sleeve and dabbing at her eyes, even though her voice was filled with emotion. "What do you propose, Lord Harlow?"

Given Christina herself did not know, she looked up at Lord Harlow expectantly, seeing how his eyes were bright with a new and fresh determination.

"As I have said, it will take a few days for such things to come completely to a satisfactory conclusion. However, there is something you must do in the meantime."

Everyone looked at Lord Harlow, and Christina held his hand tightly.

"You must marry Lady Burroughs."

Gasps of astonishment filled the room as everyone stared, completely astonished, at Lord Harlow.

"How can I do so?" Mr. Markham asked, horrified. "There are banns in place for the marriage of myself to Lady Christina, and I cannot simply—"

"A common license will do, will it not?" Lady Newfield interrupted as Mr. Markham and Lady Burroughs' eyes flared with the realization of what she meant. "You have both been residing in London for four weeks, yes? And whilst Lord Fulham will not be present to give his consent, I do not think it will be needed." She smiled warmly at Lady Burroughs. "And you yourself do not need consent, Lady Burroughs, since you have already been wed, and a note of your husband's death will be in the records already."

Lady Burroughs began to smile, and the joy in her expression made Christina want to laugh with happiness.

"And, of course, I shall be glad to be a witness," Lord Harlow said firmly.

"As will I," Lady Newfield agreed. "The marriage can take place very quickly, indeed, and certainly, there is no need to wait. It is not as though there is any other impediment."

Lord Harlow nodded. "And by the time the marriage has taken place, I will be quite prepared to speak to Lord Fulham and tell him all that has transpired. From then on, I can assure you that there will be no more difficulty between yourself and your father, Mr. Markham. And there certainly will be no demands on you to marry Lady Christina."

Christina laughed as Lady Burroughs and Mr. Markham stared at each other, their eyes wide with astonishment, only for Lady Burroughs to begin to smile and then to laugh, before throwing her arms about Mr. Markham's neck.

"I do not understand what you intend, Lord Harlow, but I can do nothing but agree," Mr. Markham said, his smile so broad that it lit up his face entirely. "I will make the arrangements at once."

"And you must do so without your father being aware of it, and I shall also need from you a list of every single gentleman to whom your father owes a debt," Lord Harlow stated firmly, although he was smiling at the gentleman. "Shall we attempt to meet with both himself and Lord Enfield next week? Thursday afternoon, mayhap?"

Everyone nodded their agreement, allowing Christina a long sigh of relief. It seemed as though everything had fallen into place, and she could not have been happier.

CHAPTER FOURTEEN

"Lord Enfield."

Richard bowed as Lord Enfield returned the gesture, although Richard could see the curiosity in the gentleman's eyes as he rose.

"Thank you for allowing me to see you," Richard continued as Lord Enfield gestured for him to sit down in a chair. "I know it is a little unexpected, but it is to do with your daughter."

Lord Enfield stiffened, stopping midway into grasping a glass of brandy.

"My daughter?" he repeated, turning slowly to look at Richard. "I do hope you are aware, Lord Harlow, that my daughter is at present engaged to Mr. Markham, the son of Baron Fulham."

The words sent a pang of remembered sorrow into Richard's heart, but he merely smiled and waited until Lord Enfield had given him the glass of brandy he had only just poured before sitting down opposite him.

"I am well aware that there is an agreement," he said,

as Lord Enfield frowned. "However, I am also aware that your daughter does not wish to marry Mr. Markham."

"Whereas you, I imagine, must wish to do so," Lord Enfield interrupted. "And whilst I would be very glad to entertain such an agreement, Lord Harlow, it is entirely out of my hands." Taking a large sip of his brandy, he sighed and lifted one shoulder. "I am sorry."

Richard chuckled, making Lord Enfield's brows rise in astonishment.

"I am very glad to hear you say that you would be glad to entertain such an agreement," Richard said with a grin. "And whilst your apology is generously meant, there is no need for it." His smile faded as he sat forward, becoming a little more serious. "I will be truthful with you, Lord Enfield. I am fully aware of everything that has occurred with Lord Fulham."

Lord Enfield blinked rapidly before a look of understanding washed down over his expression. "My daughter has told you everything."

"She has," Richard agreed. "She has also told me of the despicable way that Lord Fulham has attempted to force you into an agreement."

Closing his eyes, Lord Enfield let out a heavy sigh. "I would have taken the duel, Lord Harlow, if it had meant that Christina would have been kept safe from Lord Fulham's intentions. However, had I accepted, I know full well that my life would have been cut short, and who then would take care of Christina?" Shaking his head, he looked mournfully back at Richard. "The estate and title would have passed to someone who cares for none but himself. My dear Christina would have been—"

"I do not blame you in any way, Father."

Richard turned and smiled at Christina as she walked into the room, seeing how she looked fondly at her father.

"And yes, you are quite correct. Lord Harlow and I have been discussing this matter for some time because—"

Hesitating, she looked back towards Richard, who held out his hand to her, glad when she accepted at once.

"Because I have long had a love for him within my heart, Father. I want to marry Lord Harlow and not Mr. Markham." Squeezing Richard's hand, she perched herself elegantly on the edge of his chair, her nearness sending heat washing through Richard even though he knew he ought to be concentrating on the conversation at hand. "But I do not want you to duel either. Therefore, Lord Harlow has come up with an idea which will bring Lord Fulham's plans to an end."

Lord Enfield held his daughter's gaze, and Richard felt her hand tighten again on his own. If Lord Enfield was not willing to listen to such plans, then they might have a good deal more difficulty facing them. However, the questions in Lord Enfield's eyes did not linger for too long, for he eventually sighed, nodded, and looked back at Christina with a gentle smile.

"If it will bring you happiness, then I am willing to listen," he said softly. "I have already told Christina that if there were something I could do to change this situation in any way, then I would do so."

Richard smiled in relief. "I am delighted to hear you say so," he replied. "What I should inform you of, however, is that Mr. Markham is, in fact, at this very

moment, marrying a lady *other* than Lady Christina."
Waiting for a moment, he saw the astonishment ripple
across Lord Enfield's face and could not help but
chuckle, hearing Lady Christina laugh softly.

"It appears, Father, that Mr. Markham cares deeply
for Lady Burroughs, and has done so for a long time," she
told Lord Enfield. "But she does not have a lot of wealth
and thus, for various reasons, was not a suitable match."

"I see," Lord Enfield said slowly, his brow beginning
to furrow. "But what will Lord Fulham say when he
discovers it?"

"That," Richard said firmly, "is something that we
shall all discover together, Lord Enfield, for I should be
glad if you would join both myself and Lady Christina
tomorrow as we attend Lord Fulham at his home. Mr.
Markham, Lady Burroughs, and Lady Newfield will also
be present." His anticipation rose within him, and he
gave the gentleman a satisfied smile. "I can assure you
that Lord Fulham will no longer have any such demands
to make of you, Lord Enfield, and that all will end in a
most satisfactory manner."

Lord Enfield considered this for a moment, then
began to nod slowly. "Very well," he said, the corner of
his mouth turning up. "I must confess, I am surprised, but
I cannot pretend I am not glad that Mr. Markham is
removed from you, Christina."

"As am I," Lady Christina replied with such fervor
that Richard could not help but laugh.

"I think you know that I share that relief, Lord
Enfield," he replied as the older gentleman laughed.
"Although, there is one more thing I must ask of you."

Lord Enfield's smile faded away as he waited for Richard to speak.

"When you attend, Lord Enfield, I pray that you do not ask any questions that would give the impression to Lord Fulham that you are not entirely aware of all that has been undertaken," Richard said firmly. "I would be glad to explain it all to you at this moment, but I fear that, if I were to do so, you would do your utmost to try to dissuade me."

Lady Christina caught her breath, her eyes wide as she looked down at him. "Lord Harlow?" she asked, her voice quiet. "You mean to say that—"

"There is nothing to fear," he assured her. "But you must both project confidence and understanding. That way, Lord Fulham will feel entirely at a loss and without any hope of success." Satisfied, he pressed Lady Christina's hand once more. "And in a very short time, we shall be wed and contented, Lady Christina. I am certain of it."

"Good afternoon, Mr. Markham."

Striding into Lord Fulham's drawing-room, Richard bowed quickly before allowing Lady Christina, Lady Newfield, and Lord Enfield to precede him further into the room.

"Good afternoon," Mr. Markham replied, his face a little pale. "My father is out of the house at present but expects to return very shortly."

Richard nodded. "Very good, Mr. Markham." Seeing

the way that the gentleman had settled a hand on Lady Burroughs' shoulder, he smiled at her before bowing again. "And might I wish you both happiness."

Lady Burroughs' flushed but held his gaze. "I thank you, Lord Harlow. We are both very happy."

For a moment, no one said anything more. There was, of course, an air of tension in the room that Richard knew would only grow with each minute that passed before Lord Fulham arrived, but Richard was quite determined not to allow himself to give in to such feelings and instead to remain as calm as he could.

"Lady Christina," Mr. Markham said, speaking rather quickly as though he had been eager for some time to now say whatever was on his mind. "I have to apologize to you for my behavior and how I have treated you during our betrothal." His voice and gaze were steady as he continued. "I was rude and conceited and arrogant. I was entirely dismissive of your feelings and your requirements, and for that, I am very sorry indeed. I was wrapped up in all that I felt, and every time I was in your company, I could only think of how painful my heart was to be apart from Lady Burroughs, but that is not an excuse for behaving as I did."

Lady Christina held up one hand, silencing Mr. Markham. "Please, there is no need for you to say more," she said gently. "I believe that you behaved in such a way to please your father, Mr. Markham, and, whilst I am appreciative of your apology, you must not feel any guilt over such a thing. I fully understand."

Mr. Markham let out a breath of relief before bowing towards Lady Christina. "You are very understanding,

Lady Christina. I do wish you happy also, when the time comes."

Richard smiled and made to say something more, only for the door to open and, as he turned his head to look, Lord Fulham to stride into the room.

He stopped short, his mouth open as if he had been about to say something to his son only to have entirely forgotten what it was.

"Good afternoon, Lord Fulham."

Richard rose from his chair and looked straight at Lord Fulham, finding a sense of anger beginning to wrap around his heart. This was the gentleman who had brought them all so much pain, who had manipulated Lord Enfield, and who had cared nothing for Lady Christina herself. The gentleman who had brought nothing but difficulty to them all. The urge to get up and strike him was strong within Richard, but he quelled it at once. He was not a violent man and did not intend to begin to behave so now, no matter what Lord Fulham had done.

"Whatever is the meaning of this, Markham?"

Lord Fulham's voice was low and grave, his expression dark as he looked at his son. Mr. Markham rose to his feet and lifted his chin, determination settling in his features.

"Good afternoon, Father," he said as Richard moved slowly behind Lord Fulham, making certain that Lord Fulham could not simply return to the door and remove himself with any sort of ease.

"I believe I asked you a question," Lord Fulham grated, his whole body tensing as his shoulders lifted and his hands curled tightly. "What is the meaning of this?"

"In short," Mr. Markham said, his tone filling with confidence, "you have failed, Father."

Silence broke across them all as Lord Fulham took in what his son had said but giving as yet no reaction. Richard leaned one arm on the back of Lady Christina's chair and added in his words to Mr. Markham's, hoping to push away some of Lord Fulham's confidence.

"What Mr. Markham is attempting to state, Lord Fulham, is that your attempt to marry off your son to Lady Christina, who has both an excellent dowry and income, have entirely failed."

"And why is that?" Lord Fulham spat, turning around to face Richard. "There is nothing that can—"

"I am wed, Father."

The words seemed to crash down upon Lord Fulham, for he stumbled back as though he had been struck. Mr. Markham put his hand back on Lady Burroughs' shoulder, and, after a moment, she lifted her hand to settle it upon his.

"I am wed to Lady Burroughs," Mr. Markham said quietly. "Therefore, I cannot wed Lady Christina."

"And the debt you demanded cannot be fulfilled," Lord Enfield stated, sounding, Richard thought, a little amused. "This, I am sure, is not something that you ever expected?"

Lord Fulham said nothing for a moment, his gaze swiveling from Mr. Markham to Lord Enfield before going to Lady Burroughs. His face began to go a deep shade of red, but when he spoke, there was a control there that Richard had not expected.

"You know the consequences then, Markham," he said, looking directly at his son. "I have been keeping my gambling to a very few evenings, but I shall no longer do so." Turning a little, he pointed one hand out towards Lord Enfield. "And there shall be a duel between us, Lord Enfield. As a consequence of your lack of eagerness to push this marriage into fulfillment.

Richard chuckled despite himself, feeling a desperate eagerness to tell Lord Fulham precisely why such things could not occur. As he chuckled, he saw Lord Fulham move slowly towards him, anger practically spitting from his eyes, but Richard merely grinned.

"You think that you have succeeded, do you not?" he said as Lord Fulham glared at him, his lips twisted in a furious snarl. "But what you have threatened, Lord Fulham, shall not come to pass."

"And why ever not?" Lord Fulham roared, no longer in control of his anger. "If you think that you can—"

"I believe, Lord Fulham, that if you remained silent for even a *few* moments, you might gain some understanding," Lady Newfield interrupted briskly. "Do be silent."

For whatever reason, this appeared to prevent Lord Fulham from saying more—although whether or not it was from the shock of being spoken to in such a way by Lady Newfield or a desire to do as he had been asked, Richard did not know. Regardless, the man fell silent, and Richard grasped the opportunity to say more.

"I shall tell you why your plans will not succeed,"

Richard said. "I am aware of your intentions, Lord Fulham. I am aware that you bring in great debts and then throw the responsibility towards your son. I know that you are uncaring about your estate, eager to pull your family line higher in status and yet behaving in a manner that speaks of only lowliness." He saw the crimson rise in Lord Fulham's cheeks but continued to speak quickly, not allowing him to begin to defend himself. "And I am also aware of what you have done to Lord Enfield, in forcing this situation upon him. Threatening him with a duel, should he not comply, which would only leave his daughter in an even worse situation than she is at present!" He shook his head, holding back his anger with force. "You have brought great distress to the lady that I love, and it is for her sake that I have done all I can to bring you low, Lord Fulham." Taking a purposeful step forward, he held Lord Fulham's furious gaze. "And I can tell you now, Lord Fulham, that I have succeeded."

It was as though the air around them shattered into a thousand pieces, even though no one spoke. Richard could hear his own breathing, could almost feel the tension radiating from Lord Fulham and hear the questions being poured out towards him from everyone else in the room. Victory was already in his grasp, and it was now that he needed to take it.

"You have accumulated a good many debts, it seems," he continued, his voice steady, but his eyes narrowed. "You give them to your son, place his name upon the vowels and expect him, somehow, to deal with them as best he can." His lip curled. "But no more."

Mr. Markham made to take a step forward, but Richard shook his head, and the man stopped.

"I do not understand, Lord Harlow," Mr. Markham said slowly. "How can you force my father not to continue as he has been doing for so long?"

"Because," Richard replied, returning his gaze to the baron, "having discovered from you the list of men to whom Lord Fulham owes money at present, I have gone to each and every one of them and paid what is owed." Hearing the swift intake of breath from Lady Christina, he fought the urge to look at her, knowing that he had to fix his attention entirely upon Lord Fulham.

"Thus," he continued, keeping his voice low, "it is now only to me that you owe a debt, Lord Fulham. And I shall accept it from none but you."

Such was the shock on Lord Fulham's face that Richard needed to do nothing more but step back and place his hands behind his back, feeling fully in control. It had taken a great deal of effort to find and speak to each gentleman—and whilst he had still to hear from the few he had been forced to write to, given they were not in London for the Season, Richard felt quite certain that they would accept his offer. After all, which gentleman did not want the repayment of a debt, even if they did not fully understand the circumstances that such a repayment came about?

Sensing Lady Christina's eyes upon his face, he glanced down at her and smiled, aware of the glittering tears in her eyes and the way that her lip trembled. No doubt, she would have a good many questions, but, for the moment, she was doing as he had asked and remaining quite silent.

"You cannot do such a thing," Lord Fulham hissed, his brow knotted and his eyes filled with fury. "You cannot expect that such behavior will be tolerated!"

Richard lifted one shoulder and tilted his head. "What is it I have done wrong, Lord Fulham?" he asked quietly. "I am perfectly within my rights to do such a thing, and thus, I have done it. Knowing now that Mr. Markham wishes to be free of your torturous reign over his life, I have found great delight in speaking to each gentleman and hearing their assurance that they hold *you* entirely responsible for the debts. Thus, in taking on their vowels, I give the responsibility to you." His shoulder fell in a shrug. "And, should you accumulate more debts, I fully intend to take them on also."

Lord Fulham said nothing for a moment, his jaw working furiously, and then he shrugged as if he were trying to push aside all the aggravation that came with what Richard had said.

"It means nothing," he said. "I shall give the debts to my son to manage, as he has done before." With a laugh, he looked at Mr. Markham, who had gone very pale. "You shall not be able to prevent that, Lord Harlow."

Richard glanced at Mr. Markham before lifting one shoulder. "I believe, Lord Fulham, that I can." Seeing how Mr. Markham's shoulders slumped in evident relief, he continued quickly so as not to keep the fellow in suspense. "I will not accept any debts that come via Mr. Markham, Lord Fulham," he said firmly. "Should they do so, they will be returned at once as entirely unacceptable, for the debts are *your* responsibility and not that of your son's. In addition, should you insist on giving such a thing to Mr. Markham, then I shall have no other choice but to call you out, for you will have behaved in a most dishonorable fashion—and I can assure you, Lord Fulham, that I am very highly skilled with the foil and, should it come to it, an excellent marksman."

He let his words hang in the air as he waited for Lord Fulham's reaction. There was no fear in Richard's heart as he laid out his ultimatum, fully determined to do as he had stated, should it be required of him. There was always a risk with such duels, but Richard had very little expectation that it would ever come to such a thing. Lord Fulham, he was certain, was nothing more than a coward underneath all his bravado.

Lord Fulham lifted his chin, but Richard could see the defeat in his eyes.

"And if I refuse to pay your debts?" he stated with coldness wrapped around his words. "What then?" He laughed harshly, but the sound did nothing to provoke Richard's fear. "I shall leave you in debt for the rest of my days!"

"You shall not," Richard replied firmly, having expected Lord Fulham to have considered such a thing. "You are not too much of a gentleman to go to debtor's prison, Lord Fulham. If the debt is paid in installments—regularly and without fail—then you have nothing to fear. But, if you refuse to do so or if you are late with such payments, then I can assure you that I will have no hesitation but to insist that you are placed there until such a debt can be paid."

The color slowly drained from Lord Fulham's face, and Richard knew the victory was his. There was nothing more that Lord Fulham could say, nothing more that he could do to encourage—or force—Richard's hand. This was all now at an end, which meant that both Richard and Mr. Markham could find happiness with the ladies their hearts held close.

"It is at an end, Father," Mr. Markham said gravely. "There is nothing more that can be done. Your manipulations have come to naught. Your attempts to control me are now defunct. From this day forward, I intend to take my bride to my own establishment and remain there with her, never again to be in your company." The strength in his voice grew with every word, and Richard felt himself begin to relax. Lord Fulham was trapped on every side, and now all that waited for him was despair.

"I still shall have my money from Lord Enfield!" Lord Fulham cried, turning around to point at Lord Enfield, who startled violently in his chair. "In fact, I shall have my duel, Lord Enfield, for you have been unable to pay me what you promised—the hand of your daughter in marriage to my son."

Lord Enfield's mouth fell open, his eyes wide and a color creeping into his cheeks that spoke of fear.

"Enough, Father!" Mr. Markham exclaimed, but Lord Fulham was still quite determined, eager to seek even the smallest victory from this dire situation.

"I shall have my duel, Enfield," Lord Fulham spat. "You shall not refuse me in this."

"No," Richard interrupted mildly. "No, he shall not refuse you—but given he will have to defer to his second due to his weakness brought about by the difficulty placed upon him of late, I suggest you reconsider your demand, Lord Fulham."

For what was now the second time, Lord Fulham deflated slowly. His shoulders slumped, and he appeared to shrink slightly, dropping his head as he spoke in a dull, tired voice.

"You are to be his second, I presume, Lord Harlow."

"Given I am soon to be his son-in-law, of course, I am to be his second," Richard answered cheerfully. "But it is entirely your choice, Lord Fulham. Either you can seek a repayment of a debt—the money, of course, which will come to me, given what you owe—or you can choose to duel with Lord Enfield, knowing that I will be the one standing in his place." Meandering towards his chair, he sat down and shrugged. "The choice is entirely your own."

Lord Fulham let out a groan of frustration but did not lift his head. Richard saw that the man's hands were curled into tight fists, so tight that the skin was white around the knuckles, but he remained precisely where he was. There was nothing to fear from Lord Fulham now. All that there was remaining was Lord Fulham's choice.

"Give the money to Lord Harlow," Lord Fulham muttered, not even looking towards Lord Enfield but merely gesturing to him with one hand. "And now, if you will excuse me." He said nothing more but walked to the door, his steps dragging. With his head low, he threw open the door in evident anger before making his way through it, leaving a bemused footman to close the door behind his master.

Richard expected the room to erupt at any moment, but for a long time, no one said a single word. Lord Enfield was staring across the room, whilst Lady Christina was dabbing at her eyes with her handkerchief. Lady Newfield had rested her head back and closed her eyes, whilst Lady Burroughs was crying quietly into Mr. Markham's shoulder, having risen to her feet to step into his embrace. Richard sat quietly, savoring the joy that filled him as he looked about the room and knew that everything had worked out well. Of course, his greatest joy came from knowing that he could now marry Lady Christina, the lady who had captured his heart and to whom he owed so much.

"You have been very generous, Lord Harlow."

Lord Enfield's voice was quiet, rippling with unspoken emotion, and yet there was a haggard look about him. "I can never expect to repay you."

Richard rose to his feet at once and came to stand by Lady Christina's chair, putting his hand gently on her shoulder as she clutched at his arm.

"You owe me nothing, Lord Enfield," he said firmly. "To have your permission to wed Lady Christina is my only hope."

"You have it," Lord Enfield said at once, as Lady Christina leaned against Richard's arm. "You have it, my dear fellow. I could not ask for anyone better for her. I can never thank you enough for what you have done."

"Nor I," Lady Christina whispered, looking up at him. "That must have cost you a great deal of coin, Harlow."

Richard shrugged and smiled. "I had an investment

come through," he told her, recalling how, only a few days ago, he had been informed that his investment in shipping had done very well indeed. "And even if it had not, I would have spent every last penny I had ensuring that you were free from Lord Fulham, Lady Christina. For I love you desperately."

Had it not been for the others in the room, Richard would have pulled her to her feet and kissed her, hard, but as things stood, he knew he could not. Seeing the brightness of her smile and the joy in her eyes was enough for him for the moment, and he reached down to brush her cheek, knowing just how much he loved her.

"We must all thank you," Mr. Markham said a little gruffly. "I would never have had the courage nor the insight to do as has been done, Lord Harlow. To know that I can call Lady Burroughs my wife is more wonderful to me than anything I have ever experienced before."

"I thank you also," Lady Burroughs whispered, clearly too overcome to speak with any strength. "My joy is complete."

Richard waved their thanks away. "My only hope is that you find happiness together and contentment that will run through the rest of your lives," he said honestly. "For it is precisely what I hope for both myself and Lady Christina."

Christina could hardly believe that it was all over. Even now, as she stood in her father's drawing-room with Lord Harlow in the next room speaking to her father, it felt as though she was in some sort of dream. She remembered the moment Lord Fulham had walked into the room, felt the same sting of tension snaking over her skin and sending shivers down her spine. There had been so much at stake, so much she had been uncertain about, and yet, she had planted her trust solely in Lord Harlow, and had not been disappointed.

Her heart was filled with overwhelming joy at the outcome, however. To see her father freed of his guilt and shame, to see how Lady Burroughs had found the same happiness that Christina now felt, and to witness Mr. Markham standing up to his father in a way that Christina was certain he had never done before had made this particular afternoon one she would never forget. Through it all, she had felt herself all the more drawn to

Lord Harlow, seeing him almost in a new light even though she knew him very well indeed. There was a resoluteness about his character, a quiet strength and a determination that she could not help but admire. Had he not had the force of will to pull her from Lord Fulham's grip, then she might now be facing her wedding day to Mr. Markham, and her future would have been nothing other than bleak.

She shuddered.

"Christina?"

Lord Harlow's voice was gentle, and she turned towards him, reaching out to hold his hand as he stepped towards her. Her thoughts of what could have been faded away at once as she looked up into the eyes of the gentleman who had now become her secure and certain future.

"My dear Christina," he said, speaking with such tenderness that a flush ran into Christina's cheeks. "I have spoken to your father at length, for there were some matters that he did not fully comprehend." His smile grew, and the light in his eyes shone brightly. "However, now he fully understands everything and, should you be willing, the first banns will be called this Sunday." A laugh escaped him, his eyes crinkling gently at the corners. "There will be a great deal of scandal and rumor, however. I should warn you of that, in case you have any doubts about what you ought to do next."

Christina laughed softly and stepped closer into his embrace. His smile faded just a little as his arms clasped around her waist, his breath whispering gently across her cheek. "Surely, you know what my answer is already," she said eagerly. "This is all I have ever wanted. All I shall ever want." His lips touched hers gently. "I could never refuse you, my love."

"I was foolish to ignore my feelings for so long," he told her as she tilted her head back to look into his eyes. "Had I done so before, then mayhap I—"

"That is of no importance," she replied, interrupting him. "All that matters is where we are now." Her throat began to ache as she recalled just how close they had come to being separated forever. "Should you not have succeeded, then I do not know what we would have done."

"I would have stopped at nothing," he told her, his fingers brushing down her cheek before sweeping down her neck. "But now we are to wed, and nothing can prevent our happiness."

Christina swallowed hard, her heart filling with a renewed love for the gentleman before her. He had done so much, had led her forward with such determination and had given her hope when she had none. How much she owed him!

"You have given away so much for my sake," she told him, her eyes glistening with soft tears. "Your time, your wealth—and even your very self." A single tear tracked down her cheek as she remembered how he had promised to duel with Lord Fulham in place of her father. "And for you to seek Mr. Markham's happiness also was more than I could have ever expected."

Lord Harlow chuckled softly. "I would not have done

so at the first," he answered honestly, "but when I saw the affection between himself and Lady Burroughs, my heart resonated with all that they felt. I could not allow their sorrow, not when I knew all too well what such feelings did to my own heart."

Christina nodded, knowing precisely what he meant. "Lady Newfield intends to give Lady Burroughs a very generous gift for her wedding," she said, smiling. "It will be more than enough to help establish both herself and Mr. Markham as he waits to claim the title."

"Then I am all the more glad for them," he told her, his arms back about her waist. "I mean every word that I say, Christina. I love you most ardently."

His words sent fire through her veins, making her want to cry aloud with joy. When his lips found hers, when he kissed her fervently, she could do nothing but wrap her arms about his neck and lean into him. Her every joy complete, she let passion and hope and love sweep through her as he held her close. This was their shared moment, their shared joy when they knew that, together, there was nothing other than happiness laid out before them. A happiness that would take them by the hand and lead them together along a shared path, for every single moment of their life together.

I HOPE you enjoyed Lady Christina and Lord Harlow's story! Don't miss the first book in the Convenient Arrangement series, A Broken Betrothal...Lady Augusta and Lord Leicestershire's arranged marriage becomes more than just business! Check out a preview just two pages ahead!

If you have already read this series, please try another book from my backlist. One of my favorites that is so relevant to the times we are living in is A Baron's Malady

Thank you for reading and supporting my books! I hope this story brought you some escape from the real world into the always captivating Regency world. A good story, especially one with a happy ending, just brightens your day and makes you feel good! If you enjoyed the book, would you leave a review on Amazon? Reviews are always appreciated.

Below is a complete list of all my books! Why not click and see if one of them can keep you entertained for a few hours?

The Rogue's Flower
Saved by the Scoundrel
Mending the Duke
The Baron's Malady

The Returned Lords of Grosvenor Square
The Returned Lords of Grosvenor Square: A Regency
Romance Boxset
The Waiting Bride
The Long Return
The Duke's Saving Grace
A New Home for the Duke

The Spinsters Guild
A New Beginning
The Disgraced Bride
A Gentleman's Revenge
A Foolish Wager
A Lord Undone

Convenient Arrangements
A Broken Betrothal
In Search of Love
Wed in Disgrace
Betrayal and Lies

Christmas Stories
Love and Christmas Wishes: Three Regency Romance
Novellas
A Family for Christmas

Mistletoe Magic: A Regency Romance
Home for Christmas Series Page

Happy Reading!

All my love,

Rose

A SNEAK PEAK OF A BROKEN BETROTHAL

Lady Augusta looked at her reflection in the mirror and sighed inwardly. She had tried on almost every gown in her wardrobe and still was not at all decided on which one she ought to wear tonight. She had to make the right decision, given that this evening was to be her first outing into society since she had returned to London.

"Augusta, what in heaven's name...?" The sound of her mother's voice fading away as she looked all about the room and saw various gowns strewn everywhere, the maids quickening to stand straight, their heads bowed as the countess came into the room. Along with her came a friend of Lady Elmsworth, whom Augusta knew very well indeed, although it was rather embarrassing to have her step into the bedchamber when it was in such a disarray!

"Good afternoon, Mama," Augusta said, dropping into a quick curtsy. "And good afternoon, Lady Newfield." She took in Lady Newfield's face, seeing the twinkle in the lady's blue eyes and the way her lips twitched, which was in direct contrast to her mother, who was standing with her hands on her hips, clearly upset.

"Would you like to explain, my dear girl, what it is that you are doing here?" The countess looked into Augusta's face, her familiar dark eyes sharpening. Augusta tried to smile but her mother only narrowed her eyes and planted her hands on her hips, making it quite plain that she was greatly displeased with what Augusta was doing.

"Mama," Augusta wheedled, gesturing to her gowns. "You know that I must look my very best for this evening's ball. "Therefore, I must be certain that I—"

"We had already selected a gown, Augusta," Lady Elmsworth interrupted, quieting Augusta's excuses immediately. "You and I went to the dressmaker's only last week and purchased a few gowns that would be worn for this little Season. The first gown you were to wear was, if I recall, that primrose yellow." She indicated a gown that was draped over Augusta's bed, and Augusta felt heat rise into her face as the maids scurried to pick it up.

"I do not think it suits my coloring, Mama," she said, a little half-heartedly. "You are correct to state that we chose it together, but I have since reconsidered."

Lady Newfield cleared her throat, with Lady Elmsworth darting a quick look towards her.

"I would be inclined to agree, Lady Elmsworth," she said, only for Lady Elmsworth to throw up one hand, bringing her friend's words to a swift end. Augusta's hopes died away as her mother's thin brows began knitting together with displeasure. "That is enough, Augusta," she said firmly, ignoring Lady Newfield entirely. "That gown will do you very well, just as we discussed." She looked at the maids. "Tidy the rest of these up at once and ensure that the primrose yellow is left for this evening."

The maids curtsied and immediately set to their task, leaving Augusta to merely sit and watch as the maids obeyed the mistress of the house rather than doing what she wanted. In truth, the gown that had been chosen for her had been mostly her mother's choice, whilst she had attempted to make gentle protests that had mostly been ignored. With her dark brown hair and green eyes, Augusta was sure that the gown did, in fact, suit her coloring very well, but she did not want to be clad in yellow, not when so many other debutantes would be wearing the same. No, Augusta wanted to stand out, to be set apart, to be noticed! She had come to London only a few months ago for the Season and had been delighted when her father had encouraged them to return for the little Season. Thus, she had every expectation of finding a suitable husband and making a good match. However, given how particular her mother was being over her gown, Augusta began to worry that her mother would soon begin to choose Augusta's dance partners and the like so that she would have no independence whatsoever!

"I think I shall return to our tea," Lady Newfield said gently as Lady Elmsworth gave her friend a jerky nod. "I apologize for the intrusion, Lady Augusta."

"There was no intrusion," Augusta said quickly, seeing the small smile that ran around Lady Newfield's mouth and wishing that her mother had been a little more willing to listen to her friend's comments. For whatever reason, she felt as though Lady Newfield understood her reasoning more than her mother did.

"Now, Augusta," Lady Elmsworth said firmly, settling herself in a chair near to the hearth where a fire burned brightly, chasing away the chill of a damp winter afternoon. "This evening, you are to be introduced to one gentleman in particular. I want you to ensure that you behave impeccably. Greet him warmly and correctly, but thereafter, do not say a good deal."

Augusta frowned, her eyes searching her mother's face for answers that Lady Elmsworth was clearly unwilling to give. "Might I ask why I am to do such a thing, Mama?"

Lady Elmsworth held Augusta's gaze for a moment, and then let out a small sigh. "You will be displeased, of course, for you are always an ungrateful sort but nonetheless, you ought to find some contentment in this." She waited a moment as though waiting to see if Augusta had some retort prepared already, only to shrug and then continue. "Your father has found you a suitable match, Augusta. You are to meet him this evening."

The world seemed to stop completely as Augusta stared at her mother in horror. The footsteps of the maids came to silence; the quiet crackling of the fire turned to naught. Her chest heaved with great breaths as Augusta tried to accept what she had just been told, closing her eyes to shut out the view of her mother's slightly bored expression. This was not what she had expected. Coming back to London had been a matter of great excitement for her, having been told that *this* year would be the year for her to make a suitable match. She had never once thought that such a thing would be pulled from her, removed from her grasp entirely. Her father had never once mentioned that he would be doing such a thing but now, it seemed, he had chosen to do so without saying a word to her about his intentions.

"Do try to form some response, Augusta," Lady Elmsworth said tiredly. "I am aware this is something of a surprise, but it is for your own good. The gentleman in question has an excellent title and is quite wealthy." She waved a hand in front of her face as though such things were the only things in the world that mattered. "It is not as though you could have found someone on your own, Augusta."

"I should have liked the opportunity to try," Augusta whispered, hardly able to form the words she wanted so desperately to say.

"You had the summer Season," Lady Elmsworth retorted with a shrug. "Do you not recall?"

Augusta closed her eyes. The summer Season had been her first outing into society, and she had enjoyed every moment of it. Her father and mother had made it quite plain that this was not to be the year where she found a husband but rather a time for her to enjoy society, to become used to what it meant to live as a member of the *ton*. The little Season and the summer Season thereafter, she had been told, would be the ones for her to seek out a husband.

And now, that had been pulled away from her before she had even had the opportunity to be amongst the gentlemen of the *beau monde*.

"As I have said," Lady Elmsworth continued, briskly, ignoring Augusta's complaint and the clear expression of shock on her face, "there is no need for you to do anything other than dress in the gown we chose together and then to ensure that you greet Lord Pendleton with all refinement and propriety."

Augusta closed her eyes. "Lord Pendleton?" she repeated, tremulously, already afraid that this gentleman was some older, wealthy gentleman who, for whatever reason, had not been able to find a wife and thus had been more than eager to accept her father's offer.

"Did I not say?" Lady Elmsworth replied, sounding somewhat distracted. She rose quickly, her skirts swishing noisily as she walked towards the door. "He is brother to the Marquess of Leicestershire. A fine gentleman, by all accounts." She shrugged. "He is quiet and perhaps a little dull, but he will do very well for you." One of the maids held the door open, and before Augusta could say more, her mother swept out of the room and the door was closed tightly behind her.

Augusta waited for tears to come but they did not even begin to make their way towards her eyes. She was numb all over, cold and afraid of what was to come. This was not something she had even considered a possibility when it came to her own considerations for what the little Season would hold. There had always been the belief that she would be able to dance, converse, and laugh with as many gentlemen as thought to seek her out. In time, there would be courtships and one gentleman in particular might bring themselves to her notice. There would be excitement and anticipation, nights spent reading and re-reading notes and letters from the gentleman in question, her heart quickening at the thought of marrying him.

But now, such thoughts were gone from her. There was to be none of what she had expected, what she had hoped for. Instead, there was to be a meeting and an arrangement, with no passion or excitement.

Augusta closed her eyes and finally felt a sting of tears. Dropping her head into her hands, she let her emotions roar to life, sending waves of feeling crashing through her until, finally, Augusta wept.

CHAPTER ONE

Quite why he had arranged to be present this evening, Stephen did not know. He ought to have stated that he would meet Lady Augusta in a quieter setting than a ball so that he might have talked with her at length rather than forcing a quick meeting upon them both in a room where it was difficult to hear one's own voice such was the hubbub of the crowd.

He sighed and looked all about him again, finding no delight in being in the midst of society once more. He was a somewhat retiring gentleman, finding no pleasure in the gossip and rumors that flung themselves all around London during the little Season, although it was always much worse during the summer Season. Nor did he appreciate the falseness of those who came to speak and converse with him, knowing full well that the only reason they did so was to enquire after his brother, the Marquess of Leicestershire.

His brother was quite the opposite in both looks and

character, for where Stephen had light brown hair with blue eyes, his brother had almost black hair with dark brown eyes that seemed to pierce into the very soul of whomever he was speaking with. The ladies of the *ton* wanted nothing more than to be in the presence of Lord Leicestershire and, given he was absent from society, they therefore came towards Stephen in order to find out what they could about his brother.

It was all quite wearisome, and Stephen did not enjoy even a moment of it. He was not as important as his brother, he knew, given he did not hold the high title nor have the same amount of wealth as Lord Leicestershire, but surely his own self, his conversation and the like, was of *some* interest? He grinned wryly to himself as he picked up a glass from the tray held by a footman, wondering silently to himself that, if he began to behave as his brother had done on so many occasions, whether or not that would garner him a little more interest from rest of the *ton*.

"You look much too contented," said a familiar voice, and Stephen looked to his left to see his acquaintance, Lord Dryden, approach him. Lord Dryden, a viscount, had an estate near the border to Scotland and, whilst lower in title than Stephen, had become something of a close acquaintance these last two years.

"Lord Dryden," Stephen grinned, slapping the gentleman on the back. "How very good to see you again."

Lord Dryden chuckled. "And you," he said with an honest look in his eyes. "Now, tell me why you are standing here smiling to yourself when I know very well that a ball is not the sort of event you wish to attend?"

Stephen's grin remained on his lips, his eyes alighting on various young ladies that swirled around him. "I was merely considering what my life might be like if I chose to live as my brother does," he answered, with a shrug. "I should have all of society chasing after me, I suppose, although a good many would turn their heads away from me with the shame of being in my company."

"That is quite true," Lord Dryden agreed, no smile on his face but rather a look of concern. "You do not wish to behave so, I hope?"

"No, indeed, I do not," Stephen answered firmly, his smile fading away. "I confess that I am growing weary of so many in the *ton* coming to seek me out simply because they wish to know more about my brother."

"He is not present this evening?"

Stephen snorted. "He is not present for the little Season," he replied with a shrug of his shoulders. "Do not ask me what he has been doing, or why he has such a notable absence, for I fear I cannot tell you." Setting his shoulders, he let out a long breath. "No, I must look to my future."

"Indeed," Lord Dryden responded, an interested look on his face as he eyed Stephen speculatively. "And what is it about your future that you now consider?"

Stephen cleared his throat, wondering whether he ought to tell his friend even though such an arrangement had not yet been completely finalized. "I am to consider myself betrothed very soon," he said before he lost his nerve and kept such news to himself. "I am to meet the lady here this evening. Her father has already signed the papers and they await me in my study." He shrugged one shoulder. "I am sure that, provided she has not lost all of her teeth and that her voice is pleasant enough, the betrothal will go ahead as intended."

Lord Dryden stared at Stephen for a few moments, visible shock rippling over his features. His eyes were wide and his jaw slack, without even a single flicker of mirth in his gaze as he looked back at him. Stephen felt his stomach drop, now worried that Lord Dryden would make some remark that would then force Stephen to reconsider all that he had decided thus far, fearful now that he had made some foolish mistake.

"Good gracious!" Lord Dryden began to laugh, his hand grasping Stephen's shoulder tightly. "You are betrothed?" Shaking his head, he let out another wheezing laugh before straightening and looking Stephen directly in the eye. "I should have expected such a thing from you, I suppose, given you are always entirely practical and very well-considered, but I had not expected it so soon!"

"So soon?" Stephen retorted with a chuckle. "I have been in London for the last three Seasons and have found not even a single young lady to be interested in even conversing with me without needing to talk solely about my brother." His lip curled, a heaviness sitting back on his shoulders as he let out a long sigh. "Therefore, this seemed to be the wisest and the most practical of agreements."

Lord Dryden chuckled again, his eyes still filled with good humor. "I am glad to hear it," he said warmly. "I do congratulate you, of course! Pray, forgive me for my humor. It is only that it has come as something of a surprise to hear such a thing from you yet, now that I consider it, it makes a good deal of sense!" He chuckled again and the sound began to grate on Stephen, making him frown as he returned his friend's sharp look.

Lord Dryden did not appear to care, even if he did notice Stephen's ire. Instead, he leaned a little closer, his eyes bright with curiosity. "Pray, tell me," he began as Stephen nodded, resigning himself to a good many questions. "Who is this lady? Is she of good quality?"

"Very good, yes," Stephen replied, aware, while he did not know the lady's features or character, that she came from a good family line and that breeding would not be a cause for concern. "She is Lady Augusta, daughter to the Earl of Elmsworth."

Lord Dryden's eyes widened, and his smile faded for a moment. "Goodness," he said quietly, looking at Stephen as though he feared his friend had made some sort of dreadful mistake. "And you have met the lady in question?"

"I am to meet her this evening," Stephen answered quickly, wondering why Lord Dryden now appeared so surprised. "I have not heard anything disreputable about her, however." He narrowed his gaze and looked at his friend sharply. "Why? Have you heard some rumor I have not?"

Lord Dryden held up both his hands in a gesture of defense. "No, indeed not!" he exclaimed, sounding quite horrified. "No, tis only that she is a lady who is very well thought of in society. She is well known to everyone, seeks to converse with them all, and has a good many admirers." One shoulder lifted in a half shrug. "To know that her father has sought out an arrangement for her surprises me a little, that is all."

"Because she could do very well without requiring an arrangement," Stephen said slowly understanding what Lord Dryden meant. "Her father appeared to be quite eager to arrange such a thing, however." He sighed and looked all about him, wondering when Lord Elmsworth and his daughter would appear. "He and I spoke at Whites when the matter of his daughter came up."

"And the arrangement came from there?" Lord Dryden asked as Stephen nodded. "I see." He lapsed into silence for a moment, then nodded as though satisfied that he had asked all the questions he wished. "Very good. Then may I be the first to congratulate you!" Lord Dryden's smile returned, and he held out a hand for Stephen to shake. Stephen did so after only a momentary hesitation, reminding himself that there was not, as yet, a complete agreement between himself and Lord Elmsworth.

"I still have to sign and return the papers," he reminded Lord Dryden, who made a noise in the back of his throat before shrugging. "You do not think there will be any difficulty there, I presume?"

"Of course there will not be any difficulty," Lord Dryden retorted with a roll of his eyes. "Lady Augusta is very pleasing, indeed. I am sure you will have no partic-ular difficulty with her."

Stephen opened his mouth to respond, only to see someone begin to approach him. His heart quickened in his chest as he looked at them a little more carefully, seeing Lord Elmsworth approaching and, with him, a young lady wearing a primrose yellow gown. She had an elegant and slender figure and was walking in a most demure fashion, with eyes that lingered somewhere near his knees rather than looking up into people's faces. Her dark brown hair was pulled away from her face, with one or two small ringlets tumbling down near her temples, so as to soften the severity of it. When she dared a glance at him, he was certain he caught a hint of emerald green in her eyes. Almost immediately, her gaze returned to the floor as she dropped into a curtsy, Lord Elmsworth only a step or two in front of her.

"Lord Pendleton!" Lord Elmsworth exclaimed, shaking Stephen's hand with great enthusiasm. "Might I present my daughter, Lady Augusta." He beamed at his daughter, who was only just rising from what had been a perfect curtsy.

"Good evening, Lady Augusta," Stephen said, bowing before her. "I presume your father has already made quite plain who I am?" He looked keenly into her face, and when she lifted her eyes to his, he felt something strike at his heart.

It was not warmth, however, nor a joy that she was quietly beautiful. It did not chime with happiness or contentment but rather with a warning. A warning that Lady Augusta was not as pleased with this arrangement as he. A warning that he might come to trouble if he continued as had been decided. She was looking at him with a hardness in her gaze that hit him hard. There was a coldness, a reserve in her expression, that he could not escape. Clearly, Lady Augusta was not at all contented with the arrangement her father had made for her, which, in turn, did not bode well for him.

"Yes," Lady Augusta said after a moment or two, her voice just as icy as her expression. "Yes, my father has informed of who you are, Lord Pendleton." She looked away, her chin lifted, clearly finding there to be no desire otherwise to say anything more.

Stephen cleared his throat, glancing towards Lord Dryden, who was, to his surprise, not watching Lady Augusta as he had expected, but rather had his attention focused solely on Lord Elmsworth. There was a dark frown on his face; his eyes narrowed just a little and a clear dislike began to ripple across his expression. What was it that Lord Dryden could see that Stephen himself could not?

"Might I introduce Viscount Dryden?" he said quickly, before he could fail in his duties. "Viscount Dryden, this is the Earl of Elmsworth and his daughter—"

"We are already acquainted," Lord Dryden interrupted, bowing low before lifting his head, looking nowhere but at Lady Augusta. "It is very pleasant to see you again, Lady Augusta. I hope you are enjoying the start of the little Season."

Something in her expression softened, and Stephen saw Lady Augusta's mouth curve into a gentle smile. She answered Lord Dryden politely and Stephen soon found himself growing a little embarrassed at the easy flow of conversation between his friend and his betrothed. There was not that ease of manner within himself, he realized, dropping his head just a little so as to regain his sense of composure.

"Perhaps I might excuse myself for a short time," Lord Elmsworth interrupted before Lord Dryden could ask Lady Augusta another question. "Lady Elmsworth is standing but a short distance away and will be watching my daughter closely."

Stephen glanced to his right and saw an older lady looking directly at him, her sense of haughtiness rushing towards him like a gust of wind. There was no contentment in her eyes, but equally, there was no dislike either. Rather, there was the simple expectation that this was how things were to be done and that they ought to continue without delay.

"But of course, Lord Elmsworth," Stephen said quickly, bowing slightly. "I should like to sign your daughter's dance card, if I may?"

"I think," came Lady Augusta's voice, sharp and brittle, "then if that is the case, you ought to be asking the lady herself whether or not she has any space remaining on her card for you to do such a thing, Lord Pendleton."

There came an immediate flush of embarrassment onto Stephen's face, and he cleared his throat whilst Lord Elmsworth sent a hard glance towards his daughter, which she ignored completely. Only Lord Dryden chuckled, the sound breaking the tension and shattering it into a thousand pieces as Stephen looked away.

"You are quite correct to state such a thing, Lady Augusta," Lord Dryden said, easily. "You must forgive my friend. I believe he was a little apprehensive about this meeting and perhaps has forgotten quite how things are done."

Stephen's smile was taut, but he forced it to his lips regardless. "But of course, Lady Augusta," he said tightly. "Might you inform me whether or not you have any spaces on your dance card that I might then be able to take from you?" He bowed his head and waited for her to respond, seeing Lord Elmsworth move away from them all without waiting to see what his daughter would say.

"I thank you for your kind consideration in requesting such a thing from me," Lady Augusta answered, a little too saucily for his liking. "Yes, I believe I do have a few spaces, Lord Pendleton. Please, choose whichever you like." She handed him her dance card and then pulled her hand back, the ribbon sliding from her wrist as he looked down at it. She turned her head away as if she did not want to see where he wrote his name, and this, in itself, sent a flurry of anger down Stephen's spine. What was wrong with this young lady? Was she not glad that she was now betrothed, that she would soon have a husband and become mistress of his estate?

For a moment, he wondered if he had made a mistake in agreeing to this betrothal, feeling a swell of relief in his chest that he had not yet signed the agreement, only for Lord Dryden to give him a tiny nudge, making him realize he had not yet written his name down on the dance card but was, in fact, simply staring at it as though it might provide him with all the answers he required.

"The country dance, mayhap," he said, a little more loudly than he had intended. "Would that satisfy you, Lady Augusta?"

She turned her head and gave him a cool look, no smile gracing her lips. "But of course," she said with more sweetness than he had expected. "I would be glad to dance with you, Lord Pendleton. The country dance sounds quite wonderful."

He frowned, holding her gaze for a moment longer before dropping his eyes back to her dance card again and writing his name there. Handing it back to her, he waited for her to smile, to acknowledge what he had given her, only for her to sniff, bob a curtsy and turn away. Stephen's jaw worked furiously, but he remained standing steadfastly watching after her, refusing to allow himself to chase after her and demand to know what she meant by such behavior. Instead, he kept his head lifted and his eyes fixed, thinking to himself that he had, most likely, made a mistake.

"I would ascertain from her behavior that this betrothal has come as something of a shock," Lord Dryden murmured, coming closer to Stephen and looking after Lady Augusta with interest. "She was less than pleased to be introduced to you, that is for certain!"

Stephen blew out his frustration in a long breath, turning his eyes away from Lady Augusta and looking at his friend. "I think I have made a mistake," he said gruffly. "That young lady will not do at all! She is—"

"She is overcome," Lord Dryden interrupted, holding up one hand to stem the protest from Stephen's lips. "As I have said, I think this has been something of a shock to her. You may recall that I said I am acquainted with Lady Augusta already and I know that how she presented herself this evening is not her usual character."

Stephen shook his head, his lips twisting as he considered what he was to do. "I am not certain that I have made the wisest decision," he said softly. "Obviously, I require a wife and that does mean that I shall have to select someone from amongst the *ton,* but—"

"Lady Augusta is quite suitable," Lord Dryden interrupted firmly. "And, if you were quite honest with yourself, Lord Pendleton, I think you would find that such an arrangement suits you very well. After all—" He gestured to the other guests around him. "You are not at all inclined to go out amongst the *ton* and find a lady of your choosing, are you?"

Stephen sighed heavily and shot Lord Dryden a wry look. "That is true enough, I suppose."

"Then trust me when I say that Lady Augusta is more than suitable for you," Lord Dryden said again, with such fervor that Stephen felt as though he had no other choice to believe him. "Sign the betrothal agreement and know that Lady Augusta will not be as cold towards you in your marriage as she has been this evening." He chuckled and slapped Stephen on the shoulder. "May I be the first to offer you my congratulations."

Smiling a little wryly, Stephen found himself nodding. "Very well," he told Lord Dryden. "I accept your congratulations with every intention of signing the betrothal agreement when I return home this evening."

"Capital!" Lord Dryden boomed, looking quite satisfied with himself. "Then I look forward to attending your wedding in the knowledge that it was I who brought it about." He chuckled and then, spotting a young lady coming towards him quickly excused himself. Stephen smiled as he saw Lord Dryden offer his arm to the young lady and then step out on to the floor. His friend was correct. Lady Augusta was, perhaps, a little overwhelmed with all that had occurred and simply was not yet open to the fact that she would soon be his wife. In time, she would come to be quite happy with him and their life together; he was sure of it. He had to thrust his worries aside and accept his decisions for what they were.

"I shall sign it the moment I return home," he said aloud to himself as though confirming this was precisely what he intended to do. With a small sigh of relief at his decision, he lifted his chin and set his shoulders. Within the week, everyone would know of his betrothal to Lady Augusta and that, he decided, brought him a good deal of satisfaction.

～

His QUILL HOVERED over the line for just a moment but, with a clenching of his jaw, Stephen signed his name on the agreement. His breath shot out of him with great fury, leaving him swallowing hard, realizing what he had done. It was now finalized. He would marry Lady Augusta, and the banns would have to be called very soon, given her father wanted her wed before the end of the little Season. Letting out his breath slowly, he rolled up the papers and began to prepare his seal, only for there to come a hurried knock at the door. He did not even manage to call out for his servant to enter, for the butler rushed in before he could open his mouth.

"Do forgive me, my lord," the butler exclaimed, breathing hard from his clear eagerness to reach Stephen in time. "This came from your brother's estate with a most urgent request that you read it at once."

Startled, his stomach twisting one way and then the other, Stephen took the note from the butler's hand and opened it, noting that there was no print on the seal. His heart began to pound as he read the news held within.

"My brother is dead," he whispered, one hand gripping onto the edge of his desk for support. "He...he was shot in a duel and died on the field." Closing his eyes, Stephen let the news wash over him, feeling all manner of strong emotions as he fought to understand what had occurred. His brother had passed away, then, lost to the grave, and out of nothing more than his foolishness. To have been fighting in a duel meant that Leicestershire had done something of the most grievous nature—whether it had been stealing another man's wife or taking affections from some unfortunate young lady without any intention of pursuing the matter further.

Running one hand over his face, Stephen felt the weight of his grief come to settle on his heart, his whole body seeming to ache with a pain he had only experienced once before when their dear father had passed away. His throat constricted as he thought of his mother. He would have to go to her at once, to comfort her in the midst of her sorrow. Yes, his brother had packed her off to the Dower House long before she was due to reside there, and yes, there had been some difficulties between them, but Stephen knew that she had loved her eldest son and would mourn the loss of him greatly.

A groan came from his lips as he lifted his head and tried to focus on his butler. His vision was blurry, his head feeling heavy and painful.

"Ready my carriage at once," he rasped, "and have my things sent after me. I must return to my brother's estate."

The butler bowed. "At once," he said, his concern clear in his wide-eyed expression. "I beg your pardon for my intrusion, my lord, but is Lord Leicestershire quite well?"

Stephen looked at his faithful butler, knowing that the man had worked for the family for many years in keeping the townhouse in London readied for them and understood that his concern was genuine. "My brother is dead," he said hoarsely as the butler gasped in horror. "I have lost him. He is gone, and I shall never see him again."

CHAPTER TWO

S ix months later

AUGUSTA ROLLED her eyes as her mother brought out
the primrose yellow dress that she had worn at the start of
the little Season some six months ago. She sighed as her
mother spread it out with one hand, a look in her eye that
told Augusta she was not about to escape this easily.

"That gown was for the winter, Mama," she said,
calmly. "I cannot wear it again now that the sun is
shining and the air is so very warm." She gestured to it
with a look of what she hoped was sadness on her face.
"Besides, it is not quite up to the fashion for this current
Season."

Her mother tutted. "Nonsense, Augusta," she said
briskly. "There is very little need for you to purchase new
gowns when you are to have a trousseau. Your betrothed
has, as you know, recently lost his brother and as such,

will need to find some happiness in all that he does. I must hope that your presence will bring him a little joy in his sorrow and, in wearing the very same gown as you were first introduced to him in, I am certain that Lord Pendleton—I mean, Lord Leicestershire—will be very happy to see you again."

Augusta said nothing, silently disagreeing with her mother and having no desire whatsoever to greet her betrothed again, whether in her primrose yellow gown or another gown entirely. She had felt compassion and sympathy for his loss, yes, but she had silently reveled in her newfound freedom. Indeed, given their betrothal had not yet been confirmed and given the *ton* knew nothing of it, Augusta had spent the rest of the little Season enjoying herself, silently ignoring the knowledge that within the next few months, she would have to let everyone in the *ton* know of her engagement.

But not yet, it seemed. She had spoken to her father, and he had confirmed that the papers had not been returned by Lord Leicestershire but had urged her not to lose hope, stating that he had every reason to expect the gentleman to do just as he had promised but that he was permitting him to have some time to work through his grief before pressing him about the arrangement.

And when news had been brought that the new Marquess of Leicestershire had come to London for the Season, her father had taken it as confirmation that all was just as it ought to be. He was quite contented with the situation as things stood, silently certain that when Lord Leicestershire was ready, he would approach the Earl himself or speak directly to Augusta.

"I will not wear that gown, Mama," Augusta said frostily. "I am well aware of what you hope for but I cannot agree. That gown is not at all suitable for Lord Stonington's ball! I must find something that is quite beautiful, Mama." She saw her mother frown and tried quickly to come up with some reason for her to agree to such a change. "I know your intentions are good," she continued, swiftly, "but Lord Leicestershire will be glad to see me again no matter what I am wearing; I am sure of it. And, Mama, if I wear the primrose yellow gown, might it not remind him of the night that he was told of his brother's death?" She let her voice drop low, her eyes lowering dramatically. "The night when he had no other choice but to run from London so that he might comfort his mother and tidy up the ruin his brother left behind."

"Augusta!" Lady Elmsworth's voice was sharp. "Do not speak in such a callous manner!"

Augusta, who was nothing if not practical, looked at her mother askance. "I do not consider speaking the truth plainly to be callous, Mama," she said quite calmly. "After all, it is not as though Lord Leicestershire's brother was anything other than a scoundrel." She shrugged, turning away from her mother and ignoring the horrified look on her face. "Everyone in London is well aware what occurred."

She herself had been unable to escape the gossip and, to her shame, had listened to it eagerly at times. The late Lord Leicestershire had lost his life in a duel that had not gone well for him. He had taken a young lady of quality and attempted to steal kisses—and perhaps more—from her, only to be discovered by the young lady's brother, who was a viscount of some description. Despite the fact that such duels were frowned upon, one had taken place and the gentleman who had done such a dreadful thing to a young lady of society had paid the ultimate price for his actions. A part of her did feel very sorry indeed for the newly titled Lord Leicestershire, knowing that he must have had to endure a good deal of struggle, difficulty and pain in realizing not only what his brother had done but in taking on all the responsibilities that now came with his new title.

"I should think you better than to listen to gossip," Lady Elmsworth said, primly. "Now, Augusta, do stop being difficult and wear what I ask of you."

"No," Augusta replied quite firmly, surprising both herself and her mother with her vehemence. "No, I shall not." Taking in the look of astonishment on her mother's face, Augusta felt her spirits lift very high indeed as she realized that, if she spoke with determination, her mother might, in fact, allow her to do as she wished. She had, thus far, always bowed to her mother's authority, but ever since she had discovered that her marriage was already planned for her and that she was to have no independence whatsoever, she had found a small spark growing steadily within her. A spark that determined that she find some way to have a little autonomy, even if it would only be for a short time.

"I will wear the light green silk," she said decisively, walking to her wardrobe and indicating which one she meant. "It brings out my complexion a little more, I think." She smiled to herself and touched the fabric gently. "And I believe it brings a little more attention to my eyes."

Lady Elmsworth sighed heavily but, thankfully, she set down the primrose yellow and then proceeded to seat herself in a chair by the fire, which was not lit today given the warmth of the afternoon. "You think this is the most suitable choice, then?"

"I do," Augusta said firmly. "I shall wear this and have a few pearls and perhaps a ribbon set into my hair." Again, she smiled but did not see her mother's dark frown. "And perhaps that beautiful diamond pendant around my neck."

Lady Elmsworth's frown deepened. "You need not try to draw attention to yourself, Augusta," she reminded her sternly. "You are betrothed. You will be wed to Lord Leicestershire and he is the only one you need attempt to impress."

Augusta hid the sigh from her mother as she turned back to her wardrobe, closing the door carefully so as not to crush any of her gowns. A part of her hoped that she would not have to marry Lord Leicestershire, for given he had not yet returned the betrothal agreement to her father, there seemed to be no eagerness on his part to do so or to proceed with their engagement. Mayhap, now that he was of a great and high title, he might find himself a little more interested in the young ladies of the *ton* and would not feel the need to sign the betrothal agreement at all. It might all come to a very satisfactory close, and she could have the freedom she had always expected.

"Augusta!" Lady Elmsworth's voice was sharp, as though she knew precisely what it was Augusta was thinking. "You will make sure that all of your attention is on your betrothed this evening. Do you understand me?"

"We are not betrothed yet, Mama," Augusta replied a little tartly. "Therefore, I cannot show him any specific attention for fear of what others might say." She arched one eyebrow and looked at her mother as she turned around, aware she was irritating her parent but finding a dull sense of satisfaction in her chest. "Once the agreement has been sent to Papa, then, of course, I shall do my duty." She dropped into a quick curtsy, her eyes low and her expression demure, but it did not fool Lady Elmsworth.

"You had best be very careful with your behavior this evening, Augusta," she exclaimed, practically throwing herself from her chair as she rose to her feet, her cheeks a little pink and her eyes blazing with an unexpressed frustration. "I shall be watching you most carefully."

"Of course, Mama," Augusta replied quietly, permitting herself a small smile as her mother left the room, clearly more than a little irritated with all that Augusta had said. Augusta let a long breath escape her, feeling a sense of anticipation and anxiety swirl all about within her as she considered what was to come this evening. Lord Leicestershire would be present, she knew, for whilst he had not written to her directly to say such a thing, all of London was abuzz with the news that the new Marquess had sent his acceptance to Lord Stonington's ball. Everyone would want to look at him, to see his face and to wonder just how like his brother he might prove to be. Everyone, of course, except for Augusta. She would greet him politely, of course, but had no intention of showing any interest in him whatsoever. Perhaps that, combined with his new title and his new appreciation from the *ton,* might decide that she was no longer a suitable choice for a wife.

Augusta could only hope.

~

"GOOD EVENING, LADY AUGUSTA."

Augusta gasped in surprise as she turned to see who had spoken her name, before throwing herself into the arms of a lovely lady. "Lady Mary!" she cried, delighted to see her dear friend again. They had shared one Season already as debutantes and had become very dear friends indeed, and Augusta had missed her at the little Season. "How very glad I am to see you again. I am in desperate need of company and you have presented yourself to me at the very moment that I need you!"

Lady Mary laughed and squeezed Augusta's hand. "But of course," she said, a twinkle in her eye. "I knew very well that you would need a dear friend to walk through this Season with you—just as I need one also!" She turned and looked at the room, the swirling colors of the gowns moving all around them, and let out a contented sigh. "I am quite certain that this Season, we shall both find a suitable match, and I, for one, am eagerly looking forward to the courtship, the excitement and the wonderfulness that is sure to follow!"

Augusta could not join in with the delight that Lady Mary expressed, her heart suddenly heavy and weighted as it dropped in her chest. Lady Mary noticed at once, her joyous smile fading as she looked into Augusta's face.

"My dear friend, whatever is the matter?"

Augusta opened her mouth to answer, only for her gaze to snag on something. Or, rather, a familiar face that seemed to loom out of the crowd towards her, her heart slamming hard as she realized who it was.

"Lady Augusta?"

Lady Mary's voice seemed to be coming from very far away as Augusta's eyes fixed upon Lord Leicestershire, her throat constricting and a sudden pain stabbing into her chest. He was standing a short distance away, and even though there were other guests coming in and out of her vision, blocking her view of him entirely upon occasion, she seemed to be able to see him quite clearly. His eyes were fixed to hers, appearing narrowed and dark and filled with nothing akin to either gladness or relief upon seeing her. Her stomach dropped to the floor for an inexplicable reason, making her wonder if he felt the same about her as she did about him. Why did that trouble her, she wondered, unable to tug her gaze from his. She should be able to turn her head away from him at once, should be able to show the same disregard as she had done at their first meeting, should be able to express her same dislike for their arrangement as she had done at the first—but for whatever reason, she was not able to do it.

"Lady Augusta, you are troubling me now!"

Lady Mary's voice slowly came back to her ears, growing steadily louder until the hubbub of the room appeared to be much louder than before. She closed her eyes tightly, finally freed from Lord Leicestershire's gaze, and felt her whole body tremble with a strange shudder.

"Lady Mary," she breathed, her hand touching her friend's arm. "I—I apologize. It is only that I have seen my betrothed and I—"

"Your betrothed?"

Lady Mary's eyes widened, her cheeks rapidly losing their color as she stared at Augusta with evident concern.

"You are engaged?" Lady Mary whispered as Augusta's throat tightened all the more. "When did such a thing occur?"

Augusta shook her head minutely. "It was not something of my choosing," she answered hoarsely. "My father arranged it on my behalf, without my knowledge of it. When I was present in the little Season, I was introduced to Lord Pendleton."

"Lord Pendleton?" Lady Mary exclaimed, only to close her eyes in embarrassment and drop her head.

Augusta smiled tightly. "Indeed," she said, seeing her friend's reaction and fully expecting her to be aware of the situation regarding Lord Pendleton. "He has not signed the betrothal agreement as far as I am aware, for it has not yet been returned to my father. However, given he has been in mourning for his brother, my father has not been overly eager in pursuing the matter, believing that Lord Leicestershire—as he is now—will return the papers when he is quite ready."

Lady Mary said nothing for some moments, considering all that had been said carefully and letting her eyes rove towards where Augusta had been looking towards only a few moments before.

"That is most extraordinary," she said, one hand now pressed against her heart. "And might I inquire as to whether or not you are pleased with this arrangement?"

With a wry smile, Augusta said nothing but looked at her friend with a slight lift of her eyebrow, making Lady Mary more than aware of precisely how she felt.

"I see," Lady Mary replied, her eyes still wide but seeming to fill with sympathy as she squeezed Augusta's hand, her lips thin. "I am sorry that you have had to endure such difficulties. I cannot imagine what you must have felt to be told that your marriage was all arranged without you having any awareness of such a thing beforehand!"

"It has been rather trying," Augusta admitted softly. "I have a slight hope through it all, however."

"Oh?"

Allowing herself another smile, Augusta dared a glance back towards Lord Leicestershire, only to see him still watching her. Embarrassed, she pulled her eyes away quickly, looking back to her friend. "I have a slight hope that he might decide *not* to sign the papers," she said as Lady Mary sucked in a breath. "As he is now a marquess and an heir, what if he decides that he must now choose his bride with a good deal more consideration?" Feeling a little more relaxed, no longer as anxious and as confused as she had been only a few moments before, she allowed herself a small smile. "I might be able to discover my freedom once more."

Lady Mary did not smile. Rather, her lips twisted to one side, and her brows lowered. "But would that not then mean that your father might, once again, find you another match of his choosing?" she said quietly, as though she were afraid to upset Augusta any further. "Lord Leicestershire is certainly an excellent match, Lady Augusta. He is a marquess and will have an excellent fortune. Surely he is not to be dismissed with such ease!"

Augusta allowed herself to frown, having not considered such a thing before. She did not want to be saddled with anyone of her father's choosing, instead wanting to discover a husband of her own choice. There was that choice there that, up until the previous little Season, she had always expected to have.

"I will simply speak to my father," she said airily, trying to express some sort of expectation that her father would do precisely what she asked. "He will be willing to listen to me, I am sure."

Lady Mary's expression cleared. "Well, if that is true, then I must hope that you can extricate yourself from this...if you so wish." That flickering frown remained, reminding Augusta that she was now betrothed to a marquess. A Marquess who had influence, wealth, and a high title. Was she being foolish hoping that the betrothal would come to an end? Did she truly value her own choice so much that she would throw aside something that so many others in society would pursue with everything they had?

"I..." Augusta trailed off, looking into her friend's eyes and knowing that, with Lady Mary, she had to be honest.

"I shall consider what you have said," she agreed eventually as Lady Mary's frown finally lifted completely. "You are right to state that he *is*, in fact, a marquess, and mayhap he is not a match that I should be so eager to thrust aside."

"Might I inquire as to how often you have been in his company?" Lady Mary asked, turning to stand beside Augusta so that she might look out through the ballroom a little better. "Do you know him *very* well? Does he have a difficult personality that makes your eagerness to wed him so displeasing?"

Augusta winced as a knowing look came into Lady Mary's eyes. "I confess that I have not spent any time with him at all," she admitted, "save for our introduction and, thereafter, a country dance." She lifted one shoulder in a half shrug whilst avoiding Lady Mary's gaze. "Perhaps I have been a little hasty."

Lady Mary chuckled and nodded. "Mayhap," she agreed, with a smile that lit up her expression. "He may very well be a very fine gentleman indeed, Lady Augusta, and soon, you will be considered the most fortunate of all the young ladies present in London for the Season."

As much as Augusta did not want to accept this, as much as she wanted to remain determined to make her own choice, she had to admit that Lady Mary had made some valid considerations and she ought to take some time to think through all that had been said. It was not with trepidation but with a sense of curiosity deep within her that she walked through the ballroom with Lady Mary by her side, ready to greet Lord Leicestershire again. There was a little more interest in her heart and mind now, wondering what he would say and how he would appear when he greeted her. With a deep breath, she smiled brightly as she drew near him, her heart quickening just a little as she curtsied.

"Lord Leicestershire," she said, lifting her eyes to his and noting, with a touch of alarm, that there was not even a flicker of a smile touching his lips. "Good evening. How very good to see you again."

Lord Leicestershire frowned, his brow furrowed and his eyes shadowed. "Pardon me, my lady," he said as the other gentlemen he was talking to turned their attention towards both her and Lady Mary. "But I do not recall your name. In fact," he continued, spreading his hands, "I do not think we have ever been acquainted!"

Augusta's mouth dropped open in astonishment, her eyes flaring wide and her cheeks hot with embarrassment as she saw each of the gentlemen looking at her and then glancing at each other with amusement. Lady Mary gaped at Lord Leicestershire, her hand now on Augusta's elbow.

"If you will excuse me," Augusta croaked, trying to speak with strength only for her to practically whisper. "I must..."

"You are due to dance," Lady Mary interjected, helpfully guiding Augusta away from Lord Leicestershire. "Come, Lady Augusta."

Augusta let her friend lead her from the group, feeling utter humiliation wash all over her. Keeping her head low, she allowed Lady Mary to guide her to the opposite side of the room, silently praying that no one else was watching her. Glancing from one side to the other, she heard the whispers and laughter coming from either side of her and closed her eyes tightly, fearful that the rumors and gossip were already starting. For whatever reason, Lord Leicestershire had either chosen to pretend he did not know her or truly had forgotten her, and either way, Augusta was completely humiliated.

WHAT HAPPENS next with Lady August and Lord Leicestershire? Will they continue to fight or will they find a way to respect each other? Check out the rest of the story in the Kindle Store A Broken Betrothal